LOST™

SECRET IDENTITY

Don't miss any of the official *LOST* books
from Hyperion!

The Lost Chronicles
Lost: Endangered Species

And coming soon:
Lost: Signs of Life

LOST™

SECRET IDENTITY

CATHY HAPKA

HYPERION

NEW YORK

ISBN: 0-7868-9091-6

Hyperion books are available for special promotions and premiums. For details contact Michael Rentas, Assistant Director, Inventory Operations, Hyperion, 77 West 66th Street, 11th floor, New York, New York 10023, or call 212-456-0133.

FIRST EDITION

10 9 8 7 6 5 4 3 2 1

DEXTER OPENED HIS EYES to total darkness.

"Daisy!" he choked out, his voice sounding strange and muffled. "Daisy, where are you?"

Like a radio tuning in through static, the fuzziness inside his brain focused outward, belatedly picking up the noisy chaos all around him. Piercing screams and hoarse shouting; the clang of metal on metal; skidding and thumping and popping. And over and through and behind it all, an overriding throbbing, pulsing whine that echoed the pounding inside his head. The sounds filled him with terror, though he wasn't sure why. All he knew was that he needed to get away, to find Daisy and escape. . . .

He tried to lurch forward but was stopped short by something clutching at his body. The sensation was accompanied by a sudden dull pain around his midsection. That seemed to awaken feeling in the rest of his body, and he was assaulted by a dozen different pains from head to toe.

What was happening to him? And why couldn't he see? He blinked rapidly, but the darkness persisted even as the sounds around him grew louder. Panicked, he clawed frantically at his eyes. His fingers met a soft, yielding expanse of fabric covering his face.

He yanked it loose, already feeling foolish, and found himself blinking down at a blanket stamped with the logo of Oceanic Airlines. He'd discovered the cause of his "blindness." With that revelation, the world around him started to shift back into focus. He was sitting on the plane that was supposed to carry him back home to the United States. The binding arm holding him in place was his seatbelt, still securely fastened despite the fact that much of the plane surrounding it appeared to have disintegrated. . . .

Daisy, he thought with a new flash of panic.

It seemed to take more effort than it should have to turn his head and look at the seat beside him. When he finally managed it, he saw that the seat was empty.

He was still squinting, his eyes adjusting to the light, when a young man's anxious-looking face loomed into his view from the direction of the aisle. "Hey," the face said to him. "You all right, buddy?"

"I . . ." Dexter tried to say more, but his tongue stuck to the roof of his mouth. He swallowed hard, trying to fight back the terrifying feeling that he was looking straight up into his own face.

Then the stranger's features rearranged themselves. Dexter saw that while the young man was probably his age or perhaps a little older, the stranger really didn't look much like him at all—lighter eyes, darker hair, a different nose and chin and forehead.

"I—" Dexter began again, then stopped uncertainly. He was having trouble focusing his gaze. The other young man's tousled dark hair and concerned blue eyes swam before him like an old filmstrip seen through an aquarium.

"Hold tight," the stranger said. "We'll get you out of here in just a second."

"O—O—" Dexter paused, trying to come up with the second syllable. After a long, tiring mental struggle, it came to him. "Okay," he gasped out.

The effort of speaking had sapped him of every ounce of energy. His eyes started to droop as blackness threatened at the edges of his vision.

"Hang in there," the concerned stranger said urgently. "Stay with me, okay, buddy? Talk to me—what's your name?"

Dexter was sure he knew the answer to that question, but it seemed to be drifting somewhere just out of range. With one last burst of mental effort, he managed to reach out and reel it in.

"Dexter—Dexter Cross," he gasped out. Then he gave up and sank back into the inviting black hole of unconsciousness.

He wasn't sure how much time had passed before he woke again. Once more he found himself surrounded by darkness, but this time it was tempered by cool white moonlight and the flickering orange glow of nearby campfires. For a second or two Dexter wasn't sure where he was. Then he felt the gritty texture of sand grinding into his skin. A brisk breeze washed over him, raising goosebumps on his arms and flooding his nose with the salty, fishy, briny scent of the sea. When he lifted his arms to rub them back to warmth, his muscles screamed in protest. The motion seemed to jump-start his nervous system, as a second later his whole body erupted into a chorus of aches and pains, as if he'd been stomped on by an ill-tempered giant.

It was only then that he remembered the plane crash. His eyes closed tightly as if trying to shut out the horrific images flitting through his mind. Screaming engines, screaming people. A lurch, then another as the plane lost altitude, each drop seeming to send his guts leaping into his throat. The last thing he remembered was the way the oxygen masks had dropped and swayed back and forth. For a second he'd been afraid he wouldn't be able to grab hold of one. . . .

Dexter opened his eyes again, trying to ignore the memories. With a groan, he pushed himself upright.

"Ah, you're awake." An older man's face peered down into his. He had small but intelligent eyes and droopy, rounded cheeks that made him look a little like an old hound dog. "Hold on, I'll get Jack."

The man hurried off toward one of the fires. Dexter put a hand to his head, which felt as if it were stuffed with cotton. He wasn't sure who Jack was, or the older man, but he figured he'd find out soon enough.

In the meantime he looked around curiously. He was lying on a vast sweep of beach that glowed pale in the moonlight. When he turned his head, he saw a dense tropical jungle fading quickly into the darkness. The whole scene would have looked like an exotic resort destination on a postcard if not for the enormous chunks of charred debris littering the ground. Like ugly knife slashes on a beautiful painting, the pristine beach had been violated with jagged slabs of metal and upturned wheels and blackened engine parts. It was too dark to make out much detail, but Dexter could see a huge broken wing lying across the sand and a ruined section of fuselage sticking out of the sand like a grotesque cave.

Several large campfires were burning on the sand near the wreckage. Dozens of people huddled around the fires. A few appeared to be sleeping, though most were still awake despite the late hour. Some were talking quietly in small groups or sitting together on salvaged blankets or towels. Others were sitting or standing alone, staring at the jungle or the ocean or the sand at their feet.

How many people had been on the plane? Dexter wasn't sure, but he knew it was a lot. He started counting the survivors he could see, but he'd only reached fifteen or sixteen when he saw a tall, handsome man with close-cropped hair and a serious expression approaching him. The man was dressed in sand-spattered dark pants and a white undershirt, and his face sported several ugly-looking cuts and the beginnings of a five-o'clock shadow. Even so, there was a quiet confidence about the way he carried himself that commanded respect. Dexter felt a twinge of some emotion so fleeting he couldn't quite identify it. Anxiety? Envy? Resentment?

"Hi there," the stranger greeted him. "It's Dexter, right? I'm Jack. Arzt told me you were awake—good news. You were out for quite a while. How are you feeling?"

"A little woozy," Dexter responded truthfully.

"Well, no wonder. Looks like you were so dehydrated you passed out. You were lucky otherwise, though. I checked you over a few hours ago and everything else looks fine."

"Yeah." Dexter paused to gulp down half the bottle of water Jack handed him. "I'm prone to dehydration. Been that way since I was a kid. One time I was out on my cousin's yacht when he forgot to pack the cooler. We were almost an hour out into the bay before we noticed. My face turned bright red and he thought I was going to die. He was so panicked that he actually offered me a thousand bucks if I stayed alive until we got back to the marina." He smiled and shrugged. "That's Cousin Jay for you. He figures money can solve any problem if you have enough of it. And he does."

Jack didn't seem particularly interested in the story. He felt Dexter's forehead, then put his fingers to his wrist, checking his vital signs. "Well, you should be okay now," he said. "Just make sure to drink plenty of water and eat something if you can. There's a guy who's been collecting the food from the plane, name of Hurley. He can hook you up."

Dexter's stomach lurched at the thought of food, especially cold airplane food. "Thanks," he said. "I'm not sure eating's such a good idea right now, though."

"All right. Maybe by morning you'll have an appetite." Jack stood and brushed off his hands. "You may as well try to get some sleep before the rescuers arrive."

"Rescuers." Dexter's still-fuzzy mind latched onto the word. "Hey, why aren't they here yet? They must know we went down, right? Where are we, anyway?"

Jack shrugged. "I'm sure the rescue party is on the way. Now just try to sleep."

Dexter wanted to protest—he had more questions, important ones, if only he could remember them. . . . But it was so much easier just to lie back on the sand and relax. He stared up at the stars winking at him from between the clouds, his hand automatically creeping up to rub at the jagged, purplish scar on his chin.

"How'd you do that?" Jack asked, nodding at the scar.

Dexter blinked up at him, suddenly almost too sleepy to answer. "Fell off a horse," he answered. "I was trying to learn how to play polo, but I wasn't too good at it." He chuckled wearily. "Damn horse tossed me right into the goalpost."

Jack nodded and said, "Good night." But Dexter hardly heard him. He was already drifting off to sleep, still absentmindedly rubbing his scar.

2

"STOP PICKING AT THAT thing, boy."

Dexter yanked his hand away from his scar as his aunt Paula slapped at it irritably, the motion making the fat on her bare, sunburned upper arms jiggle. Out of the corner of his eye, Dexter saw a fellow shopper shooting them a disapproving glance.

"Sorry," Dexter mumbled. He planted both hands on the sticky plastic-coated handle of the shopping cart and kept his eyes carefully focused there, too. MONOMART MEANS AMERICAN VALUE! the garish red letters emblazoned on the cart's child safety seat screamed at him cheerfully.

"Come on this way, Dexy. I wanna see if they maybe put chips on sale for a change."

Dexter dutifully followed, pushing the cart after his aunt's lumbering form. He hated these weekly shopping trips. He hated the discount store's labyrinth of aisles with their ceiling-high shelves packed with merchandise. Just looking around at all the canned food, tacky knickknacks, and made-in-China children's wear made him dizzy, and the arctic air conditioning couldn't quite disguise the smells of cheap plastic and desperation that permeated the place. It was depressing, and if he never had to set foot in MonoMart again it would be too soon.

But his opinion didn't matter. Paula had no kids of her own, and his mother insisted that he help out. All he could do was do as they said and dream of the day he turned eighteen and could escape their clutches.

As Dexter slowed the cart to avoid running down a free-range toddler wearing nothing but a saggy diaper, Aunt Paula pulled ahead, surprisingly nimble for her bulk, and disappeared around the corner. A moment later he heard her squeal with joy from somewhere in the next aisle.

"Here we go!" she trilled triumphantly, her shrill voice carrying through the store and making several people look up in surprise. "Fifteen cents off. We better stock up—Lord only knows when this'll happen again. Where'd you get to, boy? Get over here!"

Dexter wondered dully why she was in such a good mood. As far as he knew she still hated her job at the drugstore, and according to his mother's latest rants she hadn't made any headway in squeezing more money out of her no-good ex-husband. Normally she just wandered around the store complaining about the prices, but today she seemed almost cheerful.

Following the sound of her voice, he shoved the cart past a pyramid display of canned goods that was blocking most of the aisle, nearly setting off an avalanche of creamed corn. When he looked down the next aisle, he saw that his aunt's arms were already full of bags of greasy snacks.

He pushed the cart toward her. "Let's keep up the pace here,

Dexy," she scolded as she dumped the bags in on top of the toilet paper, laundry detergent, and dish towels she'd already picked out. Her voice still sounded oddly jovial, though, with none of its normal bitterness. "We have a lot to do today." She gave him a quick pat on the arm before reaching for more snacks.

"Yo, check it out, guys. Look who's here!"

Dexter froze in place, his heart contracting with horror. Two guys and a girl his own age had just rounded the corner at the far end of the aisle. Zach Carson, Daryl Sharp, Jenna O'Malley . . . all of them part of the popular crowd at his high school, all of them from the "right" part of town. He had no idea what they were doing slumming at the MonoMart, and he didn't really care. He only wished he could sink through the floor and disappear.

The trio came strolling toward him just as Aunt Paula finished loading up the cart with junk food and headed down the aisle in their direction. Dexter winced as his three classmates pretended to squeeze against the shelves to avoid being crushed by her passing bulk. Aunt Paula didn't seem to notice, but Dexter's face burned on her behalf—and his own. Not for the first time, he wished he'd been born into an entirely different family.

His classmates were almost upon him. Dexter quickly arranged his face into a bland expression, hoping to avoid a scene.

"You here picking up some more of those stylin' T-shirts, Dex?" Daryl inquired, his eyes glittering meanly in his broad, ruddy face. He reached out with one meaty paw and Dexter flinched, expecting a blow. But Daryl only fingered Dexter's sleeve, wrinkling his nose with distaste.

Zach snorted with laughter. "Naw, man," he put in. "Dex is

probably shopping for a car. We all know he can't afford a real one, but I hear those plastic Barbie-doll cars go real cheap."

"Yeah, well you'd know, wouldn't you, Zach?" Jenna looked bored. "C'mon, are you guys finished teasing the nerd yet?" Her haughty greenish-gray eyes flicked briefly up and down Dexter's body. "Let's get some sodas and get out of here already. This place reeks."

Daryl grabbed her in an impulsive bear hug and planted a big, noisy kiss on her cheek. "Relax, babe. We're just talking to Dexter here, okay?"

"Ew." She pushed him away, swiping at her cheek. "Grow up, would you?"

"Hey! There you are. You guys trying to ditch me or something?"

Dexter glanced past the others and saw another girl approaching. She was beautiful—slim and blond, with an angelic smile and laughing blue eyes.

"Sorry, Kris," Jenna called. "I thought you were right behind us."

"'S okay." The newcomer noticed Dexter staring at her and shot him a sweet smile. "Hey, Dexter. How you doing?"

"Fine," he mumbled hoarsely, suddenly all too aware of his own shabby clothes and the cart full of cheap crap in front of him. He'd had a crush on this girl for years, though he'd never done anything about it. Girls like Kristin Vandevere just didn't go for guys like him—guys with no money, no car, no friends, no prospects.

If only he wasn't that guy . . . Dexter slipped momentarily into a familiar fantasy, one he'd spent hours concocting in Biology class while staring at the back of Kristin's blond head. In it, he became a whole different person, a sort of

SuperDexter—smooth, confident, irresistible to women. Wealthy beyond his wildest dreams, always quick with a joke or a witty story, able to leave his old, pathetic life far, far behind . . .

"So whatcha doing here, little Dexy?" Daryl's voice broke through the fantasy. "Helping your fat aunt buy extra-strength maxi pads or something?"

Dexter's whole body went rigid and his fists clenched at his sides. He could tolerate the other guys' bullying most of the time. He was used to it. But being humiliated in front of Kristin made him want to smash Daryl's self-satisfied face into a bloody pulp.

But he didn't. He couldn't. For one thing, he was the one who'd end up a bloody pulp, not big, beefy Daryl. Besides, he just wasn't like that. Confrontation wasn't his style; it was easier to let things slide off him.

"Whatever." Jenna tugged at Daryl's T-shirt. "Come on! I'm dying of boredom here."

"All right, all right. Stop your whining, woman!" But Daryl allowed her to drag him off down the aisle. The other two drifted after them. Only Kristin paused long enough to give Dexter a little wave. "See you in Bio class."

"Yeah," he croaked out, going for a jaunty, casual tone and failing miserably. "See you then."

He watched until she was out of sight around the corner. Then he sighed and closed his eyes, his whole body going limp. He leaned against the handle of the shopping cart. Why did he even bother trying? A girl like that was never going to see him as anything more than the quiet, nerdy, poor kid who sat behind her in Bio. Never, ever, ever. He might as well face it and set his sights a little lower, or . . .

CRASH!

The sudden cacophony from the next aisle startled him out of his reverie. It sounded as if the entire store was coming down over there.

Leaving the cart where it was, he hurried to see what had happened. Rounding the corner into the next aisle, the first thing he saw was a big, scattered pile of merchandise in large, colorful, flat boxes. Then he gasped as he spotted his aunt in the middle of it. She was sprawled on the floor like a beached whale, moaning and writhing and weakly trying to push several of the boxes off her chest and stomach. Her faded blue housedress was up around her thighs, exposing her flabby knees, and she had lost a shoe.

"Aunt Paula!" Dexter blurted out, rushing toward her.

He kneeled beside her, almost afraid to look into her twisted, groaning face. Instead he glanced at one of the boxes on the floor nearby. It featured a color photo of a smiling, affluent-looking man with a silvery mustache. The man was standing on the deck of a luxury yacht cooking steaks on a portable grill. Gold-colored script beside him identified him as Chef Cross, and the label on the box proclaimed that it contained one of his patented Cross Grills—as seen on TV and available at the nation's finest retailers. Dexter stared at the photo for a long moment, wishing he could transport himself onto that yacht, where Chef Cross's smile assured him that life was much more pleasant.

Meanwhile, others had heard the commotion. A middle-aged woman in a MonoMart uniform was one of the first to arrive. She skidded to a stop and looked down at Aunt Paula, wide-eyed.

"Are you okay, lady?" she asked breathlessly.

"No, I'm not okay!" Aunt Paula cried. "These boxes—the stupid display came down on me when I was just walking by. My back! Call an ambulance, someone, I can't move!"

3

IT WAS DAYLIGHT WHEN Dexter awoke again. The pains of his earlier awakening had faded to a dull, nagging, body-wide ache. He sat up, stretching his sore muscles. Someone had rigged up a tarp over him while he slept; it cast a cool blue shade over the sand, though the air was heavy with humidity and very warm.

He checked his watch, but it had stopped working. Not knowing the time made him feel disoriented; how long had it been since the crash? He could hear the chatter of voices all around him and decided it was time to find out what was going on.

The second he crawled out from beneath his makeshift shelter, the sun attacked him mercilessly. Waves of heat sizzled and rose off the sand, making him feel dizzy. Spotting the water bottle Jack had given him under the shelter, still half full, he reached down and grabbed it. The water was warm, but he gulped it down anyway. It made his head feel a little clearer—and at the same time put his stomach into a growling, snapping spasm of hunger.

Food. He needed food. That would help him think.

He remembered Jack saying something about someone collecting food from the plane. Last night, the very thought of an unheated, greasy airline meal had nauseated him. Now, though, it sounded downright appetizing. It was funny, he thought, how quickly a change of circumstance could lead to a change in perspective.

Dexter glanced around the beach. So far nobody was paying him any notice. People were walking along the shoreline, wandering amidst the wreckage, or dragging luggage and other items here and there. An overweight guy with curly hair was digging through a large suitcase, while nearby a young boy was kicking at the sand, looking dejected. Both of them looked vaguely familiar, and Dexter recalled that they'd been sitting near him on the plane.

Just behind him, someone spoke suddenly in a language Dexter didn't understand. Turning, he saw an Asian man standing there holding a black tray containing four small white dishes.

"Excuse me?" Dexter blurted out, startled by the man's sudden appearance.

The man repeated his undecipherable comment, gesturing urgently at his tray with his free hand. Taking a closer look, Dexter saw that each dish on the tray held a bit of slimy grayish substance that he assumed had once been some sort of sea life. He took a step backward as a fishy smell drifted toward him on the light sea breeze.

Once again the man spoke, sounding frustrated. He carefully pointed to one of the pieces and then mimed eating it.

Dexter shuddered. As hungry as he was, he wasn't quite *that* hungry. In fact, he was pretty sure he'd resort to eating the sand underfoot before he'd put that icky-looking thing in his mouth.

He'd never managed to develop a taste for sushi. The first time he'd tried to eat it, he'd barely made it to the restroom in time.

"No thanks," he told the man, waving his hands. The motion made another wave of dizziness pass over him. "That's okay. Thanks anyway."

The man scowled at him, once more gesturing to his offering. Dexter was trying to figure out how to make the fish guy go away when, out of the corner of his eye, he suddenly noticed a group of about half a dozen people hiking purposefully across the beach toward the trees. Among them was a slender young blond woman wearing shorts and a light-colored tank top.

His heart jumped. "Daisy!" he blurted out, leaping into action and racing across the sand without a second thought for Sushi Man. "Daisy, wait! It's me—I'm okay! Daisy!"

Despite a lightheadedness that threatened to send him reeling face-first onto the sand, he caught up to the group halfway across an open area of scrubby vegetation just off the beach. Leaping the last few steps, he grabbed her by the shoulder and spun her around to face him.

"What the— Who are you? Get your hands off me, you freak!"

A pretty blond stranger was glaring at him, her eyes shooting fire. Not Daisy. Not Daisy at all.

"Oh!" Dexter wheezed, already sweaty and out of breath from the brief run. "Sorry. I—I thought you were someone else."

"I *wish* she was someone else," one of the other people in the group muttered.

Dexter blinked at the dark-haired young man who had just spoken, wondering why he looked so familiar. Had he been sitting in his section of the flight as well?

Then, in a flash, it came back to him: This was the stranger who had helped him right after the crash, the one he'd thought was his double staring down at him. As it turned out, the two of them really didn't look that much alike other than being within a few years of the same age and having similar coloring.

He felt awkward, as if he should say something, though the other guy didn't seem to remember him. Before he could figure out what to do, the pretty blonde spoke again.

"Shut up, Boone," she snapped, tossing her head and glaring at the dark-haired stranger. "In case you haven't figured it out, I'm not exactly thrilled to be stuck here with you right now, either. That doesn't mean I'm going to whine about it all day like a big baby."

"Whatever, Shannon." Boone scowled at her, then turned away.

"Are you okay?" One of the others, a tall young woman with reddish-brown hair pulled up in a bun, was staring at Dexter with concern. "You look a little pale."

"I'm okay." Dexter forced a smile. "Sorry for the mix-up."

They continued on their way and he wandered back to the beach, feeling a bit embarrassed. He had been so certain that blond girl was Daisy. . . .

Daisy.

The name exploded in his heart, filling him with guilt. How could he have forgotten about Daisy? All this time he'd been lying around sleeping when she could be hurt . . . or worse.

"Hey, man. You all right?"

Dexter looked up, realizing he'd been wandering along staring at the ground and had almost run into someone. The speaker, an African-American man with a close-cropped goatee, was staring at him with concern.

"S-sorry," Dexter said, realizing he was still a little

light-headed. "Guess I wasn't looking where I was going. Sorry about that."

"No problem. Aren't you the guy who was passed out all night? My boy was wondering if you'd ever wake up. My name's Michael, by the way."

Glancing down the beach toward the kid he'd noticed earlier, Dexter guessed this must be the boy's father. "I'm Dexter. Dexter Cross. And yeah, I guess that was me. I'm awake now, though. And I need to find somebody—my girlfriend, Daisy." He turned his head to look around the beach, and swayed woozily.

"Whoa." Michael put out a hand to steady him. "You don't look too good, man. Are you sure you shouldn't lie down again for a while?"

"I'll be okay. I just need some food, and to find Daisy. . . ."

"Food. Right." Michael glanced around. "That big guy—Hurley—he's the food man around here. He's busy helping Jack right now, I think. But the food's over there; come on. . . ."

Before long Michael had set him up with a packet of airline food. Dexter sat in the shade of a piece of wreckage just long enough to wolf it down, barely tasting it. Then he drank down a full bottle of water.

The food and water cleared his mind. Once he was feeling better, he still could only focus on one thing: finding Daisy. He stood up and scanned the survivors he could see, but there was no sign of her.

Of course not, he told himself, scratching absently at a mosquito bite. *If she were here—and okay—she would have found me by now.*

A couple of young men walked past carrying a pile of seat cushions from the plane. Dexter stepped forward to intercept them.

"Hey," he called. "Where are the injured people? You know—from the crash. I need to find someone."

One of the young men wiped the sweat from his brow. "Hope it's not the dude with the shrapnel," he said. "The doc's with him now—not looking too good from what I hear."

"Chill, Scott," the second guy said. "You don't have to scare him." He glanced at Dexter. "It's not the dude with the shrapnel, is it?"

"It's not a dude at all," Dexter said. "It's a girl—my girlfriend, Daisy. Pretty, about this tall . . ." He held up a hand to indicate her height. "Blond hair."

The other two guys shrugged in unison. "Haven't seen anyone like that among the wounded," Scott replied. "Sorry. You could check the tents, though." He waved one hand to indicate the little colony of tarps and other temporary shelters dotted here and there amidst the wreckage.

"Okay, thanks." Dexter stepped back, shading his eyes with his hand as they went on their way. He headed for the first of the shelters, peering inside. Instead of Daisy, he found only a middle-aged man with half his leg ripped away.

With a shudder, he moved on before the man could open his eyes and see him. He checked a few more shelters, but most were empty.

As he looked around for the next spot to check, Dexter noticed a familiar-looking hound-faced man stepping out of the jungle at beach's edge. It was the guy who had called Jack for him last night, Dexter realized.

He walked toward him, planning to thank him for watching over him while he was passed out. Before he reached him, the older man spotted him approaching and did a double take.

"Hey! How did you get back here so fast?" he demanded, hurrying forward.

Dexter stared at him, confused. "What?"

"Come on," the man said. "If you know a shortcut back to the beach, spill it."

"I—I don't know what you're talking about," Dexter stammered. "My name's Dexter Cross, and I was just coming to thank you for—"

"Okay, and my name's Arzt, and nice to meet ya." The man, Arzt, peered at him rather suspiciously. "But I'm not sure what you're trying to pull here, Cross."

"Pull? I don't know what you mean."

"Sure you do," Arzt insisted. "Look, I just saw you out there by the twisted trees, okay? I know you saw me, too—you even waved, for God's sake. I know it was you; I was pretty surprised to see you up and about after being passed out for most of the past day."

Dexter shook his head. "Sorry, but you must be mistaken. I wasn't out in the jungle. I've been right here on the beach since I woke up."

Arzt looked unconvinced, but he shrugged. "If you say so." He glanced over his shoulder at the tree waving gently in the breeze. "I've been sticking pretty close to the beach myself, 'specially after whatever that was we heard last night and earlier today."

"What do you mean?" Dexter was impatient to continue his search for Daisy, but he was curious about Arzt's words—and the fearful expression that had suddenly appeared in the man's eyes. "What did you hear?" He pointed to himself. "Passed out, remember?"

"Oh, yeah." Arzt smiled briefly. "Right. Well, be glad you

missed it—it was pretty freaky. Big crashing noises, weird woo-woo noises . . ." He waved his arms around dramatically, apparently at a loss for words to illustrate what he was trying to describe.

Dexter shook his head. "But what do you mean? What was making the noises? Was it a rescue party?"

"I'm thinking that's a no." Arzt shrugged. "Nobody knows what it was. Sounded big and scary; that's all I know."

"Oh." Dexter was rapidly losing interest. Whatever Arzt was talking about, it didn't seem nearly as important as looking for Daisy. "Look, I need to find my girlfriend. Have you seen any blond girls out in the jungle? About this tall?" Dexter motioned with his hands.

"Nope. Your girlfriend, eh? You been with her long?"

"About six months or so," Dexter replied, drifting back toward the main part of the beach with Arzt beside him. "We go to college together."

"Oh yeah? What are you studying in college, Cross?"

"Psychology," Dexter replied. "I really like it. Just declared a few months ago."

"Good, good. Very interesting subject. Just take my advice—don't go into teaching. At least not ninth graders." Arzt shuddered and rolled his eyes. "Trust me on that one, I'm a teacher myself. High school science."

Dexter laughed politely. "I haven't really thought too much yet about what I'm going to do after I graduate," he admitted. "I figure I have plenty of time to decide—maybe go to grad school, maybe just take some time off to see what comes along. I guess I'm lucky that way, you know? It's nice knowing I'll always have my family's money to fall back on. . . ."

4

"YOU CAN'T HELP BEING born poor, Dexter." The school counselor, a plump, earnest, shiny-faced woman named Mrs. Washington, leaned back in her chair and crossed her hands on her lap as she gazed at him kindly. "But you *can* help what happens to you from here on out. That's where I come in. We need to talk about your plans—all your teachers are assuming you want to go to college."

Dexter shifted his weight in the uncomfortable wooden chair. Outside the window, which was closed, he could hear the muffled shouts and laughter of his schoolmates and the dull bounce, bounce, bounce of a basketball against the pavement out in the student parking lot. Inside Mrs. Washington's cramped beige office, the air was stale and nearly silent, only the droning buzz of the wall clock filling the space when she wasn't talking.

"I don't know," he mumbled after a moment. "I'm not sure college is, you know, for me. All those loans . . ."

When Mrs. Washington smiled, she looked a little like a chipmunk. A chipmunk with glasses.

"I understand your concern, Dexter," she said. "But scholarships and loans were made for students just like you. With your excellent SAT scores and grades, I expect you'll have no trouble finding scholarship money. I can help you with that. And once you're accepted at a school, you can work out a good financial aid package to cover the rest of your expenses. As successful as you're bound to be, you'll be able to pay it off in no time."

Dexter kept a polite half-smile on his face as she rambled on about tuition expenses, need-based scholarships, and more. But he wasn't really listening. If there was one thing his hardscrabble life had taught him, it was to be realistic and not get his hopes up or try to change things he couldn't control. Even with scholarships and financial aid, there just wouldn't be enough money for college. He'd long since accepted that and was trying to make the best of it. But Mrs. Washington, with her reams of information and her well-meaning, encouraging eyes, wasn't making it easy for him this time. He stared at the stack of colorful college brochures on the corner of her desk, allowing himself a brief, wistful moment of reverie.

If only . . .

He shut down the thought before it could go any further. It was no use thinking that way. He knew what his life was—and what it wasn't. There was nothing to do but accept it.

He escaped from the meeting as soon as he could, accepting the information sheets and brochures she offered just to shut her up. The basketball game was still going on out in the parking lot, so Dexter took the side door, skirting the bushes to avoid being seen. The last thing he needed that day was a run-in with the usual bullies.

Once he was out of sight around the corner, he relaxed a little. It was bad enough that he had to walk the two miles home, since he'd missed the bus because of his meeting with the counselor. The only thing worse would be if the rich boys in their BMWs and Mustangs and Jeeps caught him and decided they were bored enough to stop and taunt him about being too poor to afford a car. The last time that had happened he'd ended up with a black eye and a reputation as a wimp, since he'd done everything he could to avoid the fight in the first place.

He skirted the park and then walked along the cracked sidewalk beside Beale Street, which led toward the poor side of town where Dexter and his mother lived in their run-down rented townhouse. When he came to the big wire trash can on the corner of Fourth, he paused just long enough to pull the college brochures out of his backpack and dump them in. He stood watching them fall down among the used tissues, tin cans, and banana skins. Then he turned away, crossed the street, and trudged toward home.

When he let himself in the back door, he found his mother and Aunt Paula sitting together at the battered card table in the kitchen. His mother was still wrapped in the shabby purple robe she always wore around the house on her day off. Aunt Paula was decked out in the thick, grayish-colored neck brace she'd worn since her accident at the MonoMart. Dexter always winced when he saw it; he was pretty sure she was faking her injuries, but he'd long since learned not to confront her about such things. No matter what he thought or said about her schemes, she would never change.

Both women had half-empty glasses on the table in front of them, and Dexter was surprised to detect the faint, sour smell of alcohol in the air. That wasn't like them; while Aunt Paula was known to partake of a six-pack now and then, Dexter's mother rarely drank at all. She considered alcohol an expensive luxury to be reserved for special occasions such as weddings and funerals.

"Dexy, honey, there you are!" His mother was all smiles as she turned to greet him. Her normally sallow cheeks were flushed and there was an uncharacteristic twinkle in her pale gray eyes.

Dexter blinked in surprise. "What's going on?" he mumbled, already feeling left out of the joke.

"Guess what, Dexy?" Aunt Paula cooed. "Great news. MonoMart settled out of court!"

"Huh?"

"MonoMart," Aunt Paula repeated impatiently. "My accident. You were there, remember?"

Dexter remembered all right. His face flushed slightly as he flashed back to that day, the embarrassment of watching the EMTs struggle to hoist his aunt's bulky figure onto the stretcher while Zach and the others giggled in the background. . . .

"They gave her almost as much as she was asking for," his mother put in eagerly, her thin voice shaking with excitement. "Can you believe that? I guess for a big company like them, it ain't worth going to court over that much."

"Yeah." Aunt Paula chortled. "Can you believe it? Enough money to live on for years, and they don't even want to fight me for it!"

A shudder of revulsion, bitter and scalding, made its way through Dexter's body. This wasn't the first time his aunt had scammed her way to good fortune. There had been the time she'd sued the builder of her house for the flooring she'd ruined, and the time she'd planted a cockroach in her salad at a local fast-food place, and, perhaps the most egregious, when she'd sued her wedding planner and each of the various other merchants and services she'd used when her husband left her a month after the big day.

But this sounded like her biggest payoff yet. He wanted to ask the amount, but he held back. He didn't want to give her the satisfaction of his curiosity. It would only reinforce her feelings of success.

And she's probably proud of herself for it, too, he thought in disgust. *She probably thinks this is the best thing she ever did, and will spend the next ten years bragging about it to anyone who'll listen.*

He hated the thought of hearing it, of witnessing her coy little smirks as she lorded it over her friends and neighbors while his mother giggled along, hoping for a few scraps of generosity in return. He hated everything that said about their family. Even more, he hated the twinge of envy he felt at the thought of all that money. It was easy to stand there and condemn her for this, but was he really any better than she was? Or was he just too much of a coward to go for it like she did?

No. I'm not like that. I'll never be like that.

Dexter's whole body was tense with the force of his loathing. He wanted to speak up, to say or do something to express what he thought of the whole situation. To let Aunt Paula and his mother know that he was onto them and that he would never, ever let himself be like them; not if he had to eat out of garbage cans and sleep on the street.

"Dexy," his aunt said, interrupting his angry thoughts. "I figured I ought to share my good fortune with the most important people in the world—my family. So I'm buying your mother a new car. . . ."

"A Cadillac!" Dexter's mother broke in, clasping her thin hands in front of her face. "Can you believe it? Me, driving a brand-new Cadillac? It's just too good to be true!"

"Nothing's too good for my favorite sister." Aunt Paula beamed at her, her eyes almost disappearing in folds of fat. "Anyway, Dexy, I was trying to think of what you'd want. I was going to buy you a fancy new car, too. . . ."

The image of zooming into the school parking lot in a shiny, low-slung foreign sports car or tricked-out SUV popped into Dexter's mind. What would those rich boys think of him then? What would Kristin Vandevere think? It was a tantalizing thought, one that made him feel warm all over as he lingered over it.

No. I don't want it. Not that way, he told himself firmly. *I can live without a car. What good will a car do me, anyway? I can walk to work, and to school when I need to. A fancy car would just be another expense, and when Aunt Paula runs through her money in a few months or a year, I'll be stuck paying for it all myself on minimum wage.*

He realized Aunt Paula was still speaking. "But then I says to myself, Dexter don't really want a car all that much. But I know what he *does* want."

How could she possibly know that? Dexter wondered, resisting the urge to roll his eyes. *She doesn't know me at—*

Her next words blew away all of his sarcastic thoughts. "He wants to go off to college," Aunt Paula announced with obvious satisfaction. "So I figure, what the hell. If that's really his thing, I s'pose I can make that dream come true. That's what family's for, right?"

Dexter's jaw dropped. He was so stunned he couldn't speak for a moment.

"Surprised, ain't you, boy?" Aunt Paula grinned at him, still looking enormously pleased with herself. "You know I ain't much for all that school stuff. But you seem to be into it, so why not? I'll loan you the money for your expenses at any college you can get into, and you can pay me back later when you're some rich, educated doctor or lawyer or whatever. Deal?"

Dexter stared at her, still mute with shock. His first instinct was to refuse. He didn't want to profit from her swindled money. More than that, he didn't want her to assume that he endorsed her way of life or approved of anything he did.

But once the initial jolt of surprise passed, he immediately recognized that what she was offering him, whether she knew it or not, was a ticket out—a road to a whole new life, one that didn't revolve around punching a clock for a pittance and stretching every penny to the breaking point. Dexter felt a flare of hope as he pictured himself wandering the campus of some misty, mythical university, meeting kind, thoughtful people who wanted to hear what he had to say. It would be a new kind of existence, interesting and easy and satisfying, far from the grim reality of his life so far. He could start over from scratch, be whoever he wanted . . . maybe even a real-life SuperDexter.

Realizing that his aunt was still gazing at him, waiting for an answer, he swallowed hard and forced a smile.

"Deal," he said.

5

"THANKS, JOANNA." DEXTER TURNED to face the woman who had just sprayed insect repellent on the back of his neck. "I really appreciate it. I tried to go into the jungle to look for Daisy but the bugs were eating me alive."

"You're welcome. Good luck finding her." The woman smiled sympathetically and tucked the bug spray back in her pocket.

Joanna wandered off. Dexter rolled up his pant legs and splashed into the surf to rinse the repellent off his hands. The water felt chilly; the temperature on the beach seemed to have dropped about twenty degrees as the sun sank toward the horizon. Up and down the beach, people were adjusting their makeshift shelters and stoking the signal fires. It would be dark soon and there was still no sign of a rescue party, which meant they would all almost certainly be spending a second night on the island.

As Dexter dried off his hands on his jeans, he saw Michael struggling along the beach under the weight of a large piece of metal. "Need some help?" Dexter offered, hurrying over and grabbing one end of the metal shard.

The man looked up gratefully. "Thanks, man," he said breathlessly. "Thought I'd try using this to rig up a better shelter for me and Walt."

"Sounds good."

Dexter hadn't spoken with Michael since their first meeting earlier that day. However, during his search for Daisy, he had gotten to know a number of his other fellow castaways. There was Arzt, of course, the short-tempered but smart science teacher who had looked after him while he was unconscious. Joanna, the outgoing surfer chick. Hurley, a big, friendly walrus of a guy. George, the loud-mouthed, likeable know-it-all. John Locke, who seemed to talk only in riddles. And Scott and Steve and Janelle and Faith and Larry and many more. And of course Jack had been around all day tending to the wounded and doing whatever else needed doing.

But there was still no sign of Daisy. Nobody had seen her, nobody knew where she might be. Dexter had been half-afraid to look at the dead bodies that still lay here and there on the beach, but when he'd finally gathered his courage to do so he'd been relieved not to find her among them.

After they set down the chunk of metal, Michael brushed off his hands and nodded gratefully at Dexter. "Thanks again, man," he said. "Hey, weren't you looking for someone earlier? You find her?"

"My girlfriend, Daisy," Dexter said. "And no, I haven't found her yet. I was just going to ask if you'd seen any pretty, blond college-age girls around here. Oh, but not that one who left earlier today with the group testing the transceiver or whatever—I already saw her. . . ."

"There's another one coming right this way." Michael nodded toward someone behind Dexter.

Dexter spun around, an eager, relieved smile already forming on his face. But instead of Daisy, he saw an enormously pregnant young blonde heading toward him. "Oh," he said, deflated. "That's not her."

He'd noticed the young woman several times—it was hard not to notice her, with her giant protruding belly—but he hadn't met her yet. To his surprise, though, the pregnant girl seemed to recognize him immediately. She hurried toward him, a surprised expression on her pretty face.

"How did you get back here so fast?" she demanded in an Australian accent. "I just saw you out in the jungle!"

Startled, Dexter flashed back to Arzt's similar accusation earlier. Did he have a look-alike on the island? If so, he hadn't seen him yet.

"Nope, wasn't me," he told the pregnant girl. "I'm Dexter, by the way."

She stuck out her hand and smiled. "Hi. I'm Claire." They shook hands, but even after they finished she couldn't seem to stop staring at him. "Are you sure that wasn't you I saw out there?" she asked after a moment, resting one hand on the swell of her belly. "I would've sworn . . ."

"Wasn't me," he assured her. "I've been right here on the beach for the past couple of hours. You can ask anyone."

"Yep. I can vouch for the last ten minutes myself," Michael put in with a grin.

She laughed. "That's all right, I believe you," she said. "Both of you. Sorry if it sounded like I didn't. It's just so weird. . . ."

"Yeah," Dexter said slowly. "It is. You're not the only person to say that kind of thing to me today." He described the earlier encounter with Arzt.

"That teacher guy?" Michael rolled his eyes and chuckled. "He seems a little, you know, tightly wound."

"Still, he seemed really convinced that it was me," Dexter said. "Maybe I really do have a twin here."

"Yeah. And apparently he's spending all his time in the jungle," Michael said.

Remembering how disoriented he'd felt at first, Dexter wondered if there might still be survivors wandering around out in the woods who hadn't even found their way to the beach yet. People like his look-alike . . . or maybe Daisy.

"You know, maybe I'll go take a look in the jungle for this guy," he said. "If he's my twin I should really meet him, right?"

"You're going out there now? Be careful." Claire looked worried. "It'll be dark soon. And you never know . . ."

She let her voice trail off. Dexter guessed she was thinking of the mysterious noise-maker the others had witnessed the previous night while he was still passed out. They all got that look on their face when they talked about it, and he couldn't help wondering just what could spook them all so much.

Shrugging off such thoughts, he said good-bye to Michael and Claire and headed for the tree line. Entering at the same spot where he'd seen Claire emerge, he wandered along a faint trail enjoying the shade and quiet and relative absence of flies. It was like an entirely different world from the hot, sandy, itchy, buzzing, wreckage-laden atmosphere of the beach.

At least it was *mostly* different. He rounded a patch of shrubs and spotted a battered suitcase stuck in the thick, twisted branches of a tree just ahead. Its latch had broken and it was half open, spilling socks and T-shirts and women's underwear down the trunk and onto the forest floor.

Dexter stared at it for a moment, wondering uneasily if it belonged to Claire or Joanna or one of the other women on the beach. Or had it been packed by someone else, a woman who hadn't made it through the crash?

With a slight shudder, he turned away. It was getting darker by the second, especially there in the shadows of the thick jungle canopy, and he knew he would have to turn back soon. First, though, he wanted to take a few more minutes to look around for signs of his mysterious double, not to mention searching for Daisy. He still couldn't shake the guilty feeling that he hadn't been doing enough to find her. Sure, he'd asked around on the beach. But what good had that done? He'd already been pretty sure he wouldn't find her there. If she'd been there, she would have been sitting at his side when he woke up, holding a water bottle to his lips and making him feel better with her smile.

The thought of her beautiful smiling face gave him the familiar feelings of happiness, desire, and awe that he'd always felt in Daisy's presence. But it also brought on a twinge of uneasiness, as if there was something about the face in his memory, some flaw or pimple, that he couldn't quite bring into focus. Knitting his brow as he walked on through a grove of ancient-looking trees, he worried over the problem like a dog with a bone. What was wrong with him? Was this just some lingering effect of dehydration? Had he hit his head in the crash and suffered a concussion that Jack hadn't noticed?

A large, buzzing insect zipped busily across the trail right in front of his nose, startling him into a halt. Following its loopy flight pattern as it continued off through the trees, he noticed with a start that he wasn't alone in this part of the forest. A young man was standing in front of a large, double-trunked tree a few yards away, his back to Dexter as he bent over something on the ground. He was dressed in jeans, sneakers, and a T-shirt almost the same shade of blue as the one Dexter was wearing.

Aha! Dexter thought with a mixture of triumph, amusement, and relief. *That explains it. Same build, same clothes . . . no wonder everyone keeps mixing us up.*

"Hey!" he called out, curious to see the other guy's face. "Excuse me. You there."

The young man turned . . . and Dexter suddenly had the brief, dizzy sensation of falling into a deep, dark pit as he saw *his own face* looking back at him.

He let out a startled yelp. His doppelganger didn't react except to stare at him curiously for a long, breathless moment.

Unable to think or even breathe, Dexter stared back. The young man's features were identical to his in every way, though on closer examination his clothes looked a bit shabbier and he might have been just a touch thinner. His face was shadowed by the trees overhead, his expression impossible to read.

Then the other Dexter turned away without a word. One step, two, and he disappeared into the leafy, dappled shadows. A second later Dexter wasn't quite sure he'd been there at all.

He was still staring at the empty spot in front of the double-trunked tree a moment or two later when he heard running footsteps behind him. He turned just in time to see Michael and his son, Walt, burst out of the trees.

"Dexter!" Michael cried. "You okay, man? I heard you yell."

For a second Dexter couldn't answer. His mouth and throat felt as dry and lifeless as the sand on the beach. Finally he swallowed hard, forcing his reluctant throat into action.

"Did you see that?" he croaked out.

"See what?" Michael's eyes darted here and there around the area, his expression nervous. "Did something attack you? Was it . . . What was it?"

"Was it Vincent?" Walt put in excitedly. He jumped forward, his whole body aquiver. "My dog? Did you see him? He's a yellow Lab."

"No." Dexter shook his head, which was still spinning. "Sorry. No dog. No attack, either. It was that guy . . ."

He paused, turning to stare at the spot where the other Dexter had stood. Michael gazed at him quizzically.

"What guy?" he asked. "There's no one here but us."

"It was a guy," Dexter explained, turning to face him. "Remember what Claire said about seeing someone who looked like me out here? Well, I just saw him, too. And he doesn't just look like me—he looks *exactly* like me! I mean, down to the last detail. Like looking in a mirror. It was freaky!"

"Really? Cool!" Walt looked fascinated.

"Yeah." Michael's face registered concern as he glanced from his son to Dexter and back again. "Cool. Freaky. Whatever. Listen, are you sure you're feeling okay? It's still hot out, and wandering around too much is a good way to get dehydrated again. . . ."

"No, I'm not hallucinating, if that's what you're thinking," Dexter insisted. "I really saw this guy—I mean it. He was standing right over there, just as real as one of these trees." He smacked the trunk of the closest tree for extra emphasis.

"All right, okay, I believe you," Michael said, though his

expression indicated that he was still skeptical. "But it's almost dark, and we should get back. You can look for your—your twin or whatever in the morning."

"I guess you're right." After one last glance, Dexter turned away, back toward the beach. "Let's go."

"I know a better way to get back," Walt spoke up. "It's a shortcut. I found it today."

Michael shot his son a slightly disapproving look, but then he nodded. "All right, lead the way."

Walt rushed forward eagerly, pushing his way through the underbrush. "This way," he called back to them. "Follow me. Or wait—maybe it was through here . . ."

His voice faded as he plunged headlong into a bamboo thicket. "Walt!" Michael called. "Are you sure you know where you're going?"

Dexter hurried forward to catch up with him. "Maybe we should just—*oof!*" His foot hit something solid and he felt himself flying forward. He caught his balance on a handy tree trunk, the rough bark scraping skin off his palm.

"You okay, man?" Michael asked, stopping and turning around.

"Yeah, I'm fine. I just tripped over a root or something." Dexter glanced down at whatever it was that had made him stumble.

When he saw it, he did a double take. Instead of a tree root or a fallen branch, a human leg was lying across the path, clad in jeans and ending in a foot encased by a white athletic shoe, its thigh disappearing into a thicket of brush that hid the rest of the body from view. Dexter felt the world tilt slightly; for that dizzy moment he was suddenly certain that this was his doppelganger, lying in wait to trip him up.

Then he regained his composure. "Yo, Michael," he called. "Check this out."

Michael cast a slightly worried glance in the direction Walt had gone, but he came back to join Dexter. "What's the— hey now!" he yelped as he spotted the leg. "What the heck is that?"

"What do you think?" Dexter shuddered. "I guess no one's found this guy yet."

Michael looked uncertain. "I guess we should pull him out or something," he said. "Maybe carry him back to the beach, or—"

The sound of running feet interrupted him, and a second later Walt careened around the corner of the trail. "Hey! Where did you guys— Whoa!" The boy's eyes widened as he took in the scene. "Is that guy dead?"

"Yeah." Michael cleared his throat. "I'm pretty sure he's dead, man."

"Come on," Dexter said grimly, recalling how long he'd been unconscious. "Let's drag him out and make sure."

Michael made Walt stand back as they brushed aside enough of the foliage to uncover a second leg. Then the two of them each grabbed a foot and pulled.

The body was surprisingly heavy. A thick swarm of flies erupted out of the brush as it emerged into sight. Panting with exertion in the humid tropical air, Dexter gave one last yank, and the body's face came into view as well. Dexter's heart stopped. "Jason?" he murmured.

It was a young man, and there was no question that he was dead. His sightless eyes stared up at the treetops, and an unpleasant smell drifted up from his mouth. His face was splattered with dried blood and one hand was missing.

"Whoa . . ." Walt whispered in fascination as he inched forward for a better look.

"Ugh," Michael said, straightening up and wiping his hands on his pants. "Poor bastard."

Dexter's stomach did an unpleasant flip-flop as he gazed more closely into the young man's twisted, bloated, yet thankfully unfamiliar face.

6

DEXTER'S STOMACH JUMPED LIKE a nervous frog as the bus pulled to the curb with a loud wheezing of brakes. It eased to a halt in front of an ivy-covered brick building on a tree-lined street.

"Here you go, darlin'," the bus driver said, glancing up and meeting his eye in her large rearview mirror. "This is your stop. Good luck, college boy."

College boy. Dexter shivered slightly at the words. He had the sudden urge to explain to the bus driver, a rail-thin older woman with a face that belied a lifetime of hard work and hard luck and too many cigarettes, that they had much more in common than she knew.

Not that she could tell by looking at him—not anymore. As he stood up, he glanced down and nervously smoothed the creases in his brand-new khaki pants. They'd cost fifty-nine dollars—more than he'd ever spent on a single item of clothing in his life before this past summer. But that wasn't the half of it. The suitcases now resting in the bus's overhead rack held more new pants along with designer shirts, several pairs of leather shoes and name-brand sneakers, new underwear and socks from an upscale department store he'd never even entered before this summer, a wool coat so expensive and luxurious that he was afraid even to think about wearing it.

At least Aunt Paula understood about the clothes, Dexter thought as he stood and reached for the bags. *Not like the tuition price . . .*

He grimaced, recalling the hours of debate: "Why can't you learn just as much at the state school?" Aunt Paula had demanded on countless occasions. "I don't see why you got your heart set on some snobby Ivy League place. Those people ain't like us, boy. You won't fit in there."

"Your aunt's being so generous, Dexy," his mother would put in timidly, her meek eyes pleading with him to let it go. "Why can't you be happy with that?"

A few times he had wondered that himself. Why not just go with the flow, let them send him to State U, and go from there? It was still a hundred times better than anything he'd ever expected.

But it wasn't good enough, and deep down inside, he knew it. For one thing, Zach Carson and several of his buddies were going to the state university. How was he supposed to escape his past with those guys reminding him of it every chance they got? It would be nothing more than a way of extending the misery of high school.

Besides, why shouldn't he try for the best education he could get now that the opportunity had presented itself? Aunt Paula had more than enough money to pay for it, and if she didn't spend it on his tuition and expenses, she'd only waste it on another big-screen TV or leather sofa or even more garish, rhinestone-encrusted clothes from the local mall. Anyway, what did he have to lose? If she got fed up and withdrew her offer, he would only be back where he was before.

But deep down inside, he knew that last part was a lie. Now that he'd caught a glimmer of escape, a breath of hope for the future, he couldn't turn back. Happiness and a whole new life were almost in his grasp now, so close he could taste them. This was his chance to start his life over.

And maybe that was the best reason of all to push for the school of his choice. If he was going to start over, he wanted to do it right. The gamble had paid off, and now here he was. He'd won; he'd been accepted to the top university in the region, and Aunt Paula had grudgingly agreed to cover his bills.

"You're paying me back for this someday, remember?" she'd grumbled as she wrote out the first tuition check. "Don't forget. You better make sure you study hard so you can get into a good med school."

Med school. That was another battle for another day. For the moment Dexter was just happy to have gotten this far. He'd even managed to convince the two women that they didn't need to drive him to school by reminding them that it was almost a three-hour trip. He shuddered at the thought of being stuck in a car with the two of them for that long. Then there was the humiliating image of pulling up to the ivy-draped gates of the university in his mother's gaudy custom-painted yellow Cadillac or Aunt Paula's monstrous gold-detailed new SUV. Of course, the vehicles were the least of it. Even worse was the thought of entering his grand new life with the two of them at his side—his mother with her wan, kicked-puppy expression and frizzy over-processed hair, his aunt barreling aggressively around in her vulgar new clothes like some kind of huge, tacky bulldozer making loud, idiotic, judgmental comments about everything she saw. . . .

Shivering at the thought of what might have been, he thanked his lucky stars that they'd agreed to drive him to the bus station and leave it at that. Then he pushed aside the past and focused on the future. He was here now, on his own, just as he'd wanted.

It was a warm August afternoon, and Dexter struggled to keep hold of all his bags as he dragged them down the sidewalk. Following the arrows on several temporary signs, he found his way to the college green just a block from the bus stop. There he paused, letting his bags drop and flexing his arm muscles as he looked around.

It was exactly how he'd imagined it. The green stretched before him, covering several city blocks, its lush grass dotted here and there with flower beds and sculptures and shade trees. Lining its edges were large brick and stone buildings glowing with the mellow patina of generations, their windows glassy eyes peering down at the activity below like benevolent, bespectacled old professors.

And everywhere he looked he saw crowds of students chatting or laughing or playing Hacky Sack or listening to boom boxes or dashing here and there. All of them looked impossibly happy and smart and wealthy and supremely confident. For a second doubt crept into his mind, seeping in and dampening his optimistic mood. What made him think these people would be any different than Zach or Daryl or the other jerks back home? For a second he wished he could take it all back, just disappear into a crack in the sidewalk before they noticed him.

Then he straightened his spine, reminding himself that he

wanted them to notice him. After all, these people didn't know anything about him. For all they knew—for all they would *ever* know—he was one of them.

Trying out a confidence he didn't quite feel yet, Dexter pasted a polite smile on his face and approached a guy his age who was leaning against a lamppost nearby reading an official-looking slip of paper.

"Excuse me," Dexter said.

The other guy glanced up. He was a preppy type, dressed in khaki shorts and a designer polo shirt that had probably cost more than Dexter's mother's monthly rent. For a second Dexter cringed before his gaze. He waited for the affluent-looking stranger to sneer and insult him, maybe call over his friends to join in the fun.

Instead the stranger returned his smile. "Yo," he said. "What's up?"

Dexter was so amazed that it took him a second to respond. "Er . . . Sorry," he stammered. "Uh, I was just looking for—for the registrar's office. I need to sign in or something, I think. . . ."

He allowed his voice to trail off, feeling foolish. So much for the smooth, confident new him. So far, SuperDexter was sounding an awful lot like Plain Old Dexter.

"No prob," the other guy said, not seeming to notice Dexter's dismay. He pointed toward one of the impressive edifices lining the green. "It's that brick building right across the lawn. I just came from there. You a freshman, too?"

"Yeah." Dexter let out a breath he hadn't even realized he was holding and smiled at the other guy. "Yeah, I am. Thanks."

"Sure. See you around."

Dexter hurried off in the direction the other guy had indicated, hardly noticing the weight of his bags anymore. *This could work!* he thought, allowing himself to believe it for the first time. *This could actually work!*

Even after finding out about the money, even after being accepted at the university, even after watching Aunt Paula write out that check . . . even after all that, he still hadn't quite dared to hope that his life was really going to change. But now . . .

As he walked slowly toward the brick building, dodging his fellow matriculants, he slipped into a happy daydream. He found himself fantasizing about a circle of friends like that guy he'd just met, about hanging out on the green with them or cramming for a big test in someone's dorm room. About crusty old professors passing out syllabi full of interesting reading material, or sitting alone in a quiet corner of the library among ancient, dusty, leather-bound volumes, almost unaware of the passage of time as he drank in the beauty of some classic of literature. About huge lecture halls packed with students hanging on a popular professor's every word, or intimate seminars where he would be forced to defend his views on politics or philosophy . . .

What about med school, boy?

His aunt's harsh, demanding voice intruded on the daydream like a bucket of cold water. Dexter shuddered, doing his best to push her aside. His mother and aunt were convinced that, now that he would be attending such a fancy, expensive college, he would make it pay off by becoming a doctor—specifically, a highly paid surgeon of some sort. They didn't seem to recall that Dexter had always struggled in his high school science classes, vastly preferring English and history. But he was trying not to worry about that until absolutely necessary.

He was distracted by such worrisome thoughts by a flash of blond hair and a merry, musical laugh. Glancing that way, he saw the most beautiful girl he'd ever seen in his life.

Blond and petite, she was talking and giggling with a friend at the edge of the sidewalk, though Dexter barely saw the second girl. His entire being was fixated on the blond girl's presence. She seemed to fill the entire green with her loveliness—her silky wheaten hair, her dancing cornflower-blue eyes, her slender, tanned limbs. . . .

He swallowed hard, realizing that his lifelong crush on Kristin what's-her-name had been child's play, mere preparation for *this* feeling. It overwhelmed him, making him feel small and unimportant but at the same time more alive than ever before. He never wanted this moment to end; never wanted to stop looking at her, adoring her, thanking his lucky stars that he'd found her at last. . . .

Just then both girls noticed him staring and gazed back at him curiously. His face flushed and he tried to turn away, but he couldn't seem to rip his gaze from the blond girl's face.

Instead he summoned up his newfound courage and stepped forward. "H-hello," he stammered.

"Hi there," she replied easily, her voice just as musical as her laugh. "What's up?"

When directed at him—at him!—her smile was almost impossibly beautiful. Dexter found himself tongue-tied. "You— uh," he said blankly.

"Spit it out, dude," said the other girl, a striking brunette, with an edge of mockery in her voice.

He ignored her, keeping his focus on the beautiful blonde. "Registrar," he blurted out at last. "Um, I'm looking for the registrar's office. Do you—do you know where it is?"

She laughed again, though unlike her friend there was no hint of scorn as she replied. "Sure," she said. "You're standing right in front of it, cutie."

Then she tossed her head and hurried off, her friend at her side. Dexter stood and watched until she disappeared into the throngs of students. Then, feeling as if he'd just discovered the meaning of life, he turned and headed up the broad cement steps of the building behind him, leaving his bags in a pile on the grass outside. He was vaguely aware that he had a giddy smile on his face, but for once he didn't care what anyone else thought. All he could think about was The Girl.

The stale air and gloomy dimness of the building lobby, along with the crush of students inside, brought him back down to earth a little. Momentarily pushing aside everything else, he focused on finding his way to the correct office. Soon he was taking his place in a long line snaking its way up to a high countertop behind which several dour-faced office workers sat peering at computer screens.

While he waited, Dexter's thoughts returned to the blond girl. Now that the first thrill of their meeting had passed, anxiety was already taking its place. The university was huge—the freshman class alone numbered in the thousands. What if he never found her again?

Panic set in for a moment. But then he reassured himself— he would find her. He would definitely find her again. After all, the new SuperDexter could do anything. . . .

"Name?"

"Huh?" Dexter blinked, suddenly realizing he'd reached the front of the line. He stared at the bored-looking man behind the counter.

"Name?" the man repeated without bothering to glance up.

"Oh. It's Dexter," Dexter said absently. "Dexter Joseph Stubbs."

7

"SO WHEN'S YOUR BABY due?" Dexter asked Claire.

She glanced up from the orange she was peeling. "About a month," she replied, swiping a stray lock of hair out of her eyes and squinting at him in the bright morning sun.

He smiled. "Wow, you must be getting excited and nervous, huh?"

"Yeah." She stared down at the orange, her hands still and her expression troubled. "I don't know whether to wish it were sooner or later, y'know? Sometimes I feel like I just want to get it all over with—the pregnancy, all the aches and pains and so forth. Then I tell myself I'm crazy, and that I'm supposed to be enjoying this time. At least that's what everyone says. Then other times I want to put it all off as long as possible, since I'm not even sure how I'm going to handle it when the baby gets here. . . ." She shook her head and forced a laugh. "I guess I'm just a nutter, that's all. Someone like me probably shouldn't even be allowed to have a baby."

"You shouldn't let yourself think that way," Dexter chided gently, sensing the anxiety in her voice and wanting to help her feel better if he could. "It's only natural to be a little freaked out when you're going through a huge life-changing thing like having a baby. Anyone would feel the same way."

"Really?" She shot him a smile that lit up her whole face, like a sunbeam breaking through clouds. "Thanks. I guess it's good to hear that once in a while."

The two of them sat in silence for a moment. All around them was the hustle and bustle of the morning routine on the beach, already becoming familiar after only a couple of days. Claire finished peeling the orange and broke it into slices. Dexter watched her, his thoughts drifting to his gruesome discovery the evening before. Seeing Jason lying there in the bushes, stiff and bloody, had brought home to him that this whole grim situation was serious and all too real. Especially since he still had no idea what had happened to Daisy.

"Dexter. Earth to Dexter?"

Dexter blinked, becoming aware that Claire was waving a slice of orange in front of his face. "Sorry," he said. "Guess I sort of spaced out there. I was just thinking . . ."

"About that body you found yesterday?" Claire said softly, finishing his sentence for him.

Dexter glanced at her in surprise. It was amazing how fast news traveled around the beach. "Yeah, I guess I was," he admitted. "It was kind of a shock."

"Here." She handed him a piece of orange, looking sympathetic. "I heard it was someone you knew. That must've been hard. I hope it wasn't anyone too special to you?"

"Not really." Dexter popped the orange into his mouth and bit down. The juice that squirted out was so sweet it made his lips pucker. "I didn't know him that well," he said after he swallowed. "It was my girlfriend's older brother—I only met him a couple of weeks ago when we all went on vacation together in Australia."

"Oh." Claire cleared her throat, looking uncertain. "Um, your girlfriend, then. Was she—was she on the plane, too?"

Dexter hesitated, then opened his mouth to answer. Before he could get the words out, he heard someone calling his name. Glancing up, he saw Jack jogging toward them.

"There you are," the doctor said, sounding harried. "I've been looking for you." Noticing Claire, he shot her a quick smile. "Feeling okay this morning?"

Claire put a protective hand on her belly. "Fine, thanks," she said. "He's been kicking again."

"Good, good." Jack returned his gaze to Dexter. His eyes looked weary and a little distracted. "Listen, Dexter, I hear you have some experience in psychology."

"What? Not really," Dexter protested, a little alarmed. "I'm just a psych major in college, that's all. A freshman. I've only had a couple of classes so far."

"Close enough," Jack said. "See, a lot of people are having trouble dealing with being here." He waved a hand to indicate the survivors going about their business up and down the beach. "No wonder, right?"

Claire laughed softly. "Yeah," she said, her hand still resting on her belly.

"Anyway, I'm too busy right now to do much about it." Jack's gaze wandered up the beach toward the infirmary tent, a makeshift shelter built out of blue and yellow tarps and bits of wreckage. Inside, Dexter knew, lay a man with a large, ugly, oozing wound in his gut. The man—nobody knew his name—had come out of the crash alive but with a jagged bit of metal jutting out of his side, and the previous day Jack had removed the shrapnel and stitched up the wound. People on the beach had been talking about the man in hushed tones all morning. Those few who had seen him didn't think he looked too good. Dexter was sure Jack was doing all he could under the circumstances, but if rescue didn't arrive soon . . .

"I know," Dexter said with a shudder. "I understand."

"So that's where you come in." Jack smiled and swiped one hand across his brow, which was dotted with sweat. "I'd appreciate it if you could talk with some of them a little—see what you can do. Can't hurt, might help, right?"

"I don't know . . ." Dexter began uncertainly, rubbing the scar on his chin. He was afraid Jack might be expecting too much from his first-year psychological training. Besides, Dexter had planned to head back into the jungle to continue his search for Daisy.

"Oh, go on, Dex," Claire encouraged. "Talking with you just now certainly made *me* feel better. You have a really nice way about you, you know. You'll make a great psychologist someday."

Dexter blushed at the compliment. "Thanks." He hesitated another moment, still thinking of Daisy. But finally he glanced at Jack and nodded. "All right. I'll try to help if I can."

"Great," Jack said.

"After all, my family's always been big into helping others," Dexter went on, trying to psych himself up for the task. "There's even a Cross Foundation dedicated to stuff like . . . like . . ." He paused, puzzled when no examples came readily to mind. "Like, um . . ." he tried again. "I—I can't remember right now. But it's good, important stuff, I know that. It's one of the most respected charitable organizations in the world. Maybe one of the biggest, too—I'm not really sure. . . ."

He frowned slightly, wondering what was wrong with him. He'd been careful to drink plenty of water to keep dehydration at bay, and his mind felt as clear as it ever had. So why couldn't he remember such a basic detail from his own life?

Finally he shook his head and let it drop. Jack didn't seem very interested in the details, anyway. He gave Dexter a short list of people he thought could use his help, then thanked him and hurried off toward the infirmary tent.

"Wow, your family has its own charity organization?" Claire commented when Jack was gone. "That's impressive."

"Yeah." Dexter shrugged. "My—my Grandfather Cross . . . no, my great-grandfather . . . one of them started it after he made his fortune in the stock market. I think."

He did his best to focus his mind and summon up the right information, annoyed with the odd gaps in his memory. How was he supposed to help other people regain their sanity when big chunks of his own mind seemed to be drifting off in space? But try as he might, the only thing he could bring to mind when he thought of the Cross Foundation was the fuzzy, inexplicable image of a paramedic pushing a stretcher.

He shook his head, frustrated with himself. "Oh well," he told Claire, pushing himself to his feet. "I'm sure it'll all come back to me. We're probably all still in shock, at least a little bit."

"Probably," she agreed.

Leaving her to finish her breakfast, Dexter headed down the beach in search of the first person on his list, a woman named

Rose. He found her sitting just above the tide line staring out
to sea.

"Hi there," he said, flopping down on the sand beside her.
"Remember me? We met yesterday—my name's Dexter."

She didn't respond. Her hand was at her throat, clutching
the necklace she was wearing. There was a faint smile on her
face, and her eyes never wavered from the horizon.

Dexter tried to get her attention a few more times, but it was
no use. She remained silent and distant, hardly seeming to
know he was there. Finally he left her, feeling a bit discouraged
by his first attempt at therapy.

Fortunately he fared better with the next couple of "pa-
tients." First he spent about twenty minutes talking with
Janelle, a nervous-eyed young woman he'd met the day before,
and by the time they parted ways he was pretty sure he'd managed to cheer her up a little. Then he spoke more briefly with
Arzt, who despite Jack's concern seemed okay to Dexter—just
cranky and sunburned.

Next on the list was Hurley, the big guy who'd taken on the
task of organizing the food and water supplies from the plane.
Over the past twenty-four hours he had also seemed to be serv-
ing as Jack's amateur nurse, spending a lot of time with him
and the injured man in the infirmary tent.

Dexter found him digging through a suitcase in the shade of
the airplane wing. "Hey," he said. "What's up?"

"Dude." Hurley glanced up at him, red-faced, panting with
exertion. "People pack some really bizarre stuff in their suitcases."

Dexter grinned. "Oh yeah?"

"Yeah." Hurley tossed his head to get his curly hair out of his
sweaty face. "Totally. I've been through these bags like three

times now looking for medicine and stuff, and you wouldn't believe what I've found."

"You're looking for medicine?" Dexter glanced toward the infirmary tent. "For that guy up there?"

"Yeah, I guess." Hurley shrugged and added in a mutter, "Not that it'll do him much good . . ."

Ignoring that, Dexter glanced down into the suitcase. "So are you finding much?"

"Not really," Hurley said with another shrug. "Jack said to look for, you know, antibiotics. But there isn't much here. I've been through everything." He waved a hand toward the piles of luggage stacked nearby. Then he swallowed hard and glanced at something over Dexter's shoulder. "Almost everything."

Dexter glanced back and realized he was staring at the fuselage. "Did you look inside there?"

Hurley nodded. "Dude. No way. Bodies."

Dexter shuddered, thinking of the crash victims still trapped inside the body of the plane. After a couple of days under the hot tropical sun . . .

"I hear you," he told Hurley, banishing the sudden, gruesome image of Daisy strapped lifeless into an airline seat while flies crawled across her blank blue eyes. "I don't blame you."

He immediately changed the subject, and the two of them discussed the anticipated rescue party and various other topics while Dexter helped Hurley dig through several more bags. But Dexter couldn't help noticing that the other guy kept glancing over at the fuselage, his normally cheerful expression darkening each time. It unnerved him a little, especially when he thought about the horrors that lay inside.

I should look for Daisy in there. The thought scampered

across his mind, unasked for and unwelcome. *What if she's in there?*

He glanced nervously up at the fuselage rising up from the sand like a burnished metallic tombstone. No. She couldn't be in there.

What if she is?

The more Dexter tried to squelch the idea, the more irrationally convinced he was that Daisy was lying in there, baking in the ovenlike metal shell of the plane. It was almost as if someone else were controlling his mind, someone rational and heartless.

She isn't on the beach, the voice insisted with cold, clear logic. *She isn't in the jungle. Where else could she be?*

"Dude. You okay? You look kind of sick or something."

Realizing that Hurley was peering at him with concern, Dexter forced a smile. "I'm okay," he said. "I think I'd better get out of the sun for a while, though."

Hurley looked sympathetic. "Good idea," he said, mopping his brow with a pair of boxer shorts he'd just pulled out of one of the suitcases. "It's brutal out here."

Dexter said good-bye and hurried toward the tree line, carefully keeping his gaze averted from the looming bulk of the fuselage. He knew all he had to do to settle his mind was go in there and take a look around. No big deal.

But somehow he just couldn't bring himself to do it. He couldn't go in there. Maybe Hurley's aversion had rubbed off on him, or maybe he just couldn't face the idea of the smell, the flies, the sadness.

I have to, he told himself. *I need to know if she's in there.*

He was so focused on trying to convince himself that he

almost crashed into Jack, who was hurrying toward him. "Sorry," Dexter blurted out.

"How's it going?" Jack asked. "There's someone else I think you should talk to—Scott got lost in the jungle, and now that he's back he's kind of freaking out about it. Do you have a minute to talk him down?"

"Sure," Dexter said, glad for any excuse to interrupt his previous train of thought. "I've got a minute for that. Definitely."

He hurried after Jack, his relief only slightly tarnished by a brief pang of guilt.

8

DEXTER GLANCED DOWN AT the class schedule in his hand, then up at the handwritten sign tacked beside the classroom door, feeling a brief pang of guilt. "Intro to British Literature," the sign read. Dexter could imagine what his aunt would say if she knew he was taking that sort of class: *Why are you wasting your time and my money on that fruity-loopy kind of garbage?* she would demand with a snort. *Use that brain everyone says you have and sign up for something useful instead. When you're a rich doctor, you can afford to buy yourself all the high-falutin' literature-type books you want.*

Dexter grimaced at the thought. Most of the classes he'd signed up for were more than practical enough to please Aunt Paula—Chemistry, Biology, Economics, Spanish. But he couldn't graduate without a few credits in the humanities. So why not take something he might actually enjoy, even if it might not pay off financially someday? He'd always loved English class in high school, devouring the books his teachers assigned before the other kids had finished complaining about having to read them.

Anyway, SuperDexter doesn't let a couple of sour old women tell him what to do, he thought rather defiantly. *SuperDexter wants to expand his mind, and he does whatever it takes to do that.*

He grinned and glanced around the crowded hallway, glad that no one could hear his thoughts. Feeling better, he stepped toward the doorway and glanced into the classroom. Inside, there was no sign of the professor yet, though about a dozen other students were already seated at the battered old built-in desks or milling around near the front of the room.

"Yo, Dex," a familiar voice called out. "How you doing, brother?"

Dexter leaned back out of the doorway and glanced down the hall. Coming toward him was Lance, a guy who lived across the hall in his dorm. Lance was a freshman, too, and had been recruited for the university's basketball team. In addition to being tall, athletic, and popular, he was one of the smartest guys Dexter had ever known. Ever since they'd met, it had been a struggle for Dexter not to fall back into his lifelong habit of being completely intimidated by people like Lance. But he was doing his best to fight that habit, and so far it seemed to be working.

"Hey, buddy," he said, his voice sounding as casual and easygoing as Lance's own. As Lance loped up to him, he held out his hand for a high five. "What's going on?"

Lance slapped his hand with a grin. "Just trying to survive the first week," he said. "Man, the professors here are brutal— I already have a paper to write and like eight chapters to read, and I've only been to one class so far today!"

Dexter chuckled. "I hear you. I think my chemistry prof is trying to kill us. Bet I'll have some reading to do for this one, too." He hooked a thumb at the sign by the classroom door. "You taking this class?"

"No way, man." Lance shook his head. "I had enough lit classes in high school. I'm taking Psych 101 for my freshman humanities requirement—way easier."

"Sounds good. I'd better get in there," Dexter said. "See you later."

"Yeah. If you want, knock on my door when you go to dinner, okay? Maybe we can head over to the dining hall together." Lance tossed him a mock salute and turned away. "Don't think too hard, brother!"

"See you." Dexter felt like a million bucks as he headed into the classroom. If someone like Lance wanted to be his friend, how much of a loser could he be? Maybe the people back home—Aunt Paula, the kids at school—had been wrong about him all these years.

He looked around for an empty seat. Just as he was about to take a spot near the back of the room, he glanced forward . . . and his heart skipped a beat. There, sitting in the front row, was the girl from the green! Her blond head was bowed over some papers on her desk, but he would have recognized her anywhere. He'd been keeping his eyes peeled for her since that first encounter a couple of days ago, but hadn't seen her. Until now.

His throat had suddenly gone dry, and he swallowed hard. This was his chance. Would he dare to take it?

What would SuperDexter do? he asked himself.

That gave him courage. Taking a deep breath, he walked forward and slipped into the empty desk beside hers.

She glanced up at him. He smiled at her.

"Hey," he said, feigning surprise. "It's you."

For a split second she looked puzzled, then her smiled widened. "Oh, yeah," she said. "The guy who couldn't find the registrar's office."

Her tone was playful rather than mean, and he laughed. "Yeah, that's me," he said. "If I'd been any closer, I would've tripped over it."

She giggled, then stuck out her hand. "I'm Daisy," she said. "Daisy Ward."

"Dexter Stubbs," Dexter responded, taking her hand. Her skin felt soft and warm to the touch, and he didn't want to let go. "Are you a freshman?"

"Yeah," she said. "English major—at least for now. My father claims I'll probably change my mind at least fifteen times before graduation." She let out one of her merry little musical laughs. "I think he's secretly hoping I'll major in Econ, just like he did when he was a student here a million years ago. What about you?"

"Freshman. Undeclared," Dexter said. "I'm thinking about—about being an English major, too." That was true, technically. He had thought about it. He just knew his aunt would never allow it, not while he was on her dime.

Forcing such gloomy thoughts out of his mind, he did his best to focus on what Daisy was saying. She was talking about her favorite authors and the classes she'd taken in high school. Before long, they were chatting about books and literature as if they'd known each other forever. Even though he'd been looking forward to this class all day, Dexter was disappointed when the professor came in and called for order.

As the class wound down an hour later, Dexter frantically searched his mind for something witty to say to Daisy to get her to stay and talk to him for a few minutes. He still barely knew anything about her, and he couldn't stand the thought of waiting until the next meeting of the literature class, two days later, to find out more.

To his surprise, she was the first one to speak after the professor dismissed the class. "So what did you think, Dexter Stubbs?" she asked. "You're not going to drop the class or anything, are you?"

"No way," he said quickly, feeling a moment of panic. He'd never even considered that possibility, but what if she had? What if she dropped the class and he never saw her again? "What about you?" he asked as casually as he could manage.

She started gathering up her notebooks and tucking them into her bag. "Nope," she said lightly. "I'm afraid you're stuck with me for the whole semester. Hope you don't mind."

"I don't mind," he choked out, overwhelmed at the realization that the most beautiful, amazing girl he'd ever met was . . . yes . . . *flirting* with him!

She smiled. "Good. Where are you going next?"

Before he quite realized what was happening, the two of them were strolling down the campus walk together on their way to a local coffee place. "So you said your dad went to school here too, right?" he said. "That's cool."

She shrugged. "I guess. Although I guess some people think I have it easy, being a legacy and all."

"A legacy?" Dexter repeated uncertainly. "What do you mean?"

"Haven't you ever heard of a legacy? It means your parents or grandparents or whatever went to this school, which means you have a much better chance of getting in. Some people think it means they have to let you in, but that's not really true."

She rolled her eyes. "Although, since my father's name is on the new business library, it can be hard to convince some people that I was accepted on my own merits."

"Really?" Dexter shot her a quick glance, not sure if she was joking.

But her face was serious. "Yeah," she said. "He donated the money to renovate it a few years ago." She shook her head, making her blond hair fall into her eyes. "But enough about me. What's your family like, Dexter? Did any of your relatives go to school here or donate any buildings or anything?"

He hesitated. She had been so open with him so far that he felt bad about hiding the truth about himself. But how could he do anything else? If she found out what he really was, that his SuperDexter exterior hid a penniless nerd, there was no way a beautiful, classy, wealthy girl like her would want to hang out with him. Besides, if word got around, that would be the end of SuperDexter for good. He would be just another charity case, like the kid on his hall who was working three jobs to stretch his financial aid package.

"Nope, no legacy here," he said at last, kicking aimlessly at a pebble on the path. "My parents both went to Princeton. They just about wrote me out of the will when they heard I wanted to come here instead." His laughter sounded amazingly normal even to himself. "Actually, I'm kidding. They're cool with it."

"What do they do?" Daisy asked. "And where do they live?"

"They're both lawyers in—in New York City." Dexter felt a twinge of uneasiness as yet another lie slipped out. How was he going to carry off that particular whopper? He had never been to New York City in his life. "Um—but I went to boarding school, so my home is, um, Connecticut," he added quickly. Daisy had mentioned earlier that her family was in Virginia, so he figured that was a safe choice.

"Really? What school?" Daisy asked with interest. Before Dexter could panic, she added, "Choate? Hotchkiss?"

"Yeah," he blurted out, relieved. "Um, I mean, the second one—Hotchkiss."

"Oh, okay. I know tons of people from Choate, but only one guy who went to Hotchkiss. He worked for my father—he'd be at least four or five years ahead of you," she said. "You probably don't know him—Jackson Halloway?"

Dexter shook his head. "Never heard of him," he said truthfully.

She asked him a few more questions about himself after that and he managed to answer all of them without slipping up. In fact, he was a little surprised at how easily the stories slipped off his tongue . . . not to mention how easily she believed them.

His Aunt Paula would have said that was because most people were born suckers. But Dexter preferred to think of it in a different way. Maybe his newly invented version of himself was so successful so far because that was who he was truly meant to be. If he could believe in SuperDexter, he could become him.

He smiled to himself as they reached the coffee shop and he held the door for Daisy to step inside. Yes, he liked that theory. He liked it a lot.

9

DEXTER WAS SITTING ON a piece of wreckage chatting with Scott and his buddy, Steve, when there was a shout from the edge of the jungle. "They're back!" cried an older man Dexter didn't know, waving his arms. "They're back!"

"Who's back?" Dexter wondered, squinting in that direction.

"Must be the transceiver patrol," Steve said.

Scott stood up for a better look. "Guess that means whatever's out there didn't get 'em after all." He glanced at Dexter. "Steve wanted to take bets on how many of them actually made it back in one piece."

All around them, people were murmuring and staring and hurrying closer for a better look. Hurley wandered over, his arms full of water bottles. "Dudes," he greeted Dexter and the others. "What's all the commotion about?"

"Sounds like the transceiver hikers are back," Scott told

him. "You know, Sayid and Kate and the rest. Someone just saw them coming this way."

"No way." Hurley stared wide-eyed toward the jungle's edge. "Dude, I thought those guys were goners when they didn't come back last night."

"Me, too," Steve said.

Dexter stood and stretched, keeping his gaze trained on the edge of the woods. A moment later, six figures appeared there, including the blonde he'd mistaken for Daisy along with the auburn-haired woman, the young guy named Boone, and three other men. They all looked tired and sweaty but otherwise fine.

Hurley let out a loud gasp. "Yo, it's true!" he shouted. "They're back! Hey, someone should tell Jack!"

Apparently deciding he should be the one to do that, he dropped the bottles he was holding in the sand and took off across the beach. Meanwhile Steve and Scott rushed forward with the rest of the onlookers to greet the six. Dexter trailed along behind them, absentmindedly rubbing his scar. Several people had told him about the group that had gone hiking up the mountain in search of a signal for the transceiver someone had found in the broken plane's cockpit, and he had already figured out that it must have been that same group he'd interrupted shortly after awakening the day before. As he watched the blond girl—Shannon, one of her companions had called her— he felt a flush of embarrassment at the way he'd grabbed her, thinking she was Daisy. Now that he got a better look at her, he realized it was no wonder he'd made that mistake. She really did look a lot like his girlfriend, though she appeared to be a few years older.

"Attention, everyone!" The man at the head of the returning

group, a handsome, dark-skinned Middle Eastern type, looked around at the gathering crowd. "We'll tell you all about the trip in just a moment. Let's gather over there so everyone can hear."

He pointed to a central spot and marched toward it. Most of the others followed. As Shannon walked past Dexter, she did a double take.

"Hey," she said, pushing back a lock of hair that the breeze was blowing into her face. "It's that guy who assaulted me yesterday."

Dexter smiled weakly. "Yeah, it's me," he said. "Sorry about that."

The dark-haired young guy, Boone, stopped too. He glanced from Shannon to Dexter and back again. "Look, don't start giving some poor innocent guy a hard time just because you're in a bad mood, Shannon."

She rolled her eyes. "Get a sense of humor, Boone," she snapped. "I was just kidding around. You knew that, right?" She turned to gaze at Dexter with a winning little smile.

"Yeah, sure." Dexter shrugged. "No biggie. I'm Dexter, by the way. And I really am sorry for grabbing you like that. I thought you were my girlfriend."

"Oh yeah?" Shannon's eyes sparkled with mischief. "Thought I was your girl, hmm? I've heard that one before."

Dexter blushed. "No!" he said. "My girlfriend Daisy. You—you look a lot like her."

"Don't let her get to you, man," Boone said with a sigh. "If there's one thing my sister loves, it's teasing men."

"Your sister?" For some reason Dexter had assumed the two of them were a couple. But now that he thought about it, siblings made much more sense. They certainly bickered like brother and sister.

"Yeah. Lucky me, huh?" Boone rolled his eyes as Shannon smacked him on the arm. Then he glanced up the beach. "Come on, we'd better go—Sayid's getting ready to speak."

Dexter trailed along after them as they hurried toward the crowd gathering around the dark-haired Middle-Eastern guy, Sayid. Even though the two of them were clearly in the middle of some kind of spat, he liked them both already. Maybe it was because Shannon looked so much like Daisy. Or maybe it was because Boone, despite being a few years older, reminded him of his own college buddies. Either way, he was glad they'd turned up.

Dexter sped up when he realized Sayid was already speaking. People were still running from all directions to join the small group surrounding him.

"As you and the others know," Sayid announced, "we hiked up the mountain in an attempt to help the rescue team locate us. The transceiver failed to pick up a signal. We weren't able to send out a call for help."

There was a faint murmur of disappointment from the group. Dexter felt his own heart sink. Ever since hearing about the transceiver project, he'd taken it for granted that they would soon be rescued.

"But we're not giving up," Sayid went on. "If we gather electronic equipment—the cell phones, laptops—I can boost the signal and we can try again. But that may take some time, so for now we should begin rationing our remaining food. If it rains, we should set up tarps to collect water. I need to organize three separate groups. Each group should have a leader. One group for water—I'll organize that. Who's going to organize electronics? . . ."

He went on to talk about rationing food and constructing

shelters, but Dexter had stopped listening. Sayid's words were bringing home the gravity of their situation. Rationing food? Collecting rainwater? It was as if, up until now, Dexter had been going along thinking this was some sort of vaguely uncomfortable adventure, like summer camp for grown-ups. But now he was forced to face the fact that it was real, and that the rescuers everyone kept waiting for didn't seem to be showing up, and nobody knew what was going to happen next.

And that meant he had to accept that something else was all too real, too. Daisy was still nowhere to be found.

As Sayid continued to talk, Dexter glanced toward the looming bulk of the fuselage. Even in the bright sunlight it looked somehow dark and ominous, as if the spirits of the deceased still trapped inside were oozing out into the sunny day.

I should go in there, Dexter told himself, biting his lip. *I should go look for Daisy. If she's in there, it's better to know . . .*

He shuddered as a series of images popped into his head and starting playing out like a movie reel, completely beyond his control. He saw Daisy's limp figure still strapped into its plush blue airplane seat. For a moment everything around her was as still as death, only the buzzing flies giving life to the scene. But then, movement. A shadowy figure entered from somewhere—Dexter wasn't sure where—and leaned over Daisy's motionless form, peering intently into her face. Then the figure glanced up, as if staring straight toward Dexter. And Dexter saw that the shadowy figure wore his own face . . .

He shuddered and rubbed his eyes, chasing away the images. What was wrong with him? First the weird doppelganger sighting in the jungle, and now these disturbing hallucinations about Daisy . . .

"Hey, Lester."

Dexter started, suddenly noticing that the older man named George was standing in front of him. He also realized that Sayid's speech was over and the castaways were breaking into work groups.

"It's Dexter," he said.

"Sorry, Dexter." George grinned apologetically. "Sayid needs a couple more guys to help with the water set-up. You in?"

"Sure." Dexter was relieved to have a reason to stop thinking about Daisy and his own newly erratic mind. "Let's go."

It was a breezy day and the tarps were difficult to control, tending to flap and blow around at the least opportune time. Before long all of them were hot and sweaty, and Dexter had to stop several times to gulp water.

"Dude," Hurley commented at one point, watching him drain the last drops out of a bottle. "Save some for the rest of us, okay?"

Feeling a pang of guilt, Dexter opened his mouth to apologize. But Arzt, who was tying down a tarp nearby, spoke up for him.

"Let him alone, big guy," the science teacher told Hurley. "He's the one who spent the first day here unconscious from being badly dehydrated. So unless you want him passing out on us again, give it a rest."

"Oh, yeah." Hurley grinned sheepishly at Dexter. "Sorry about that, dude, I forgot. Drink away." But as he turned away, Dexter just barely heard him add in a mutter, "I just hope it rains soon."

It didn't take long for Hurley to get his wish. The castaways had hardly finished tying down the last of the tarps when the sky opened up, releasing a drenching tropical downpour.

Dexter quickly ducked under the overhang of a large sheet of metal. All over the beach, people were racing around frantically seeking whatever shelter they could find from the deluge.

Squinting out into the rain, Dexter spied Boone and Shannon peering around for a dry spot. "Guys!" he shouted, waving to them. "In here! There's plenty of room!"

Boone spotted him and gestured to his sister. Then the two of them raced across the open sand, heads down against the driving rain. A moment later they burst into Dexter's hideaway, breathless and dripping.

"Thanks, man," Boone panted, clapping Dexter wetly on the shoulder. "That storm came out of nowhere."

"Yeah." Dexter glanced out. The rain was so heavy that it obscured any sight of people or wreckage more than about four feet away. "But at least we got all the tarps set out, so we should have plenty of water after this."

"That's good news, anyway," Boone agreed.

Boone and Shannon had been in a different work group from Dexter, so the three of them traded news for the next few minutes as the rain continued. Now that it appeared that a rescue party might not arrive as quickly as first expected, food and water were the main concerns on everyone's mind.

"Luckily, it looks like there's plenty of fruit in the jungle," Boone commented. "And that Korean guy was passing out some kind of seafood yesterday, so there's that."

Shannon wrinkled her nose. "It may come from the sea and be technically edible," she said. "But it's not exactly the sushi bar at Matsuhisa."

"Beggars can't be choosers, sweetheart," Boone told her.

"Oh, shut up. Don't tell me you're not jonesing for your favorite table at that new steakhouse you love so much." Shannon stared at Boone with an evil glint in her eye. "Just think—a big, juicy porterhouse, medium-rare . . ."

"You're killing me here." Boone glanced at Dexter. "She's talking about Carnivour, by the way. If you've spent any time in LA in the past year I'm sure you know it, right?"

"I've been to LA a million times." Dexter paused, trying to dredge up any association with the restaurant he'd mentioned. "Carnivour, did you say? Actually I—I don't think I've heard of that one."

"Really?" Shannon looked surprised. "What are you, a vegetarian or something? I can't believe you haven't been there. *Everyone's* been there."

Dexter shrugged. "Yeah," he said slowly, still searching his brain for any hint of familiarity. "I hear you. I feel like I should know it, you know? But it's like I just can't quite remember. Like that part of my brain is closed off or something."

"Don't sweat it, Dex," Boone said, leaning back and squeezing water out of his shirt hem. "All our brains are fried these days. No wonder, after what we've just been through."

"True." Dexter smiled, feeling slightly better immediately. "Anyway, speaking of good food, Daisy and I tried this amazing place while we were in Sydney . . ."

As rain continued to pound the beach outside, the three of them chatted easily. Despite their frequent outbursts of squabbling, Dexter found Boone and Shannon to be smart, interesting, and easy to talk to—a lot like his friends back at school. Hanging out with people who spoke his language and got his jokes—people who were like him—made him feel a little more comfortable in this strange, foreign, scary place.

10

JUST A FEW WEEKS into the first semester, Dexter was already growing more comfortable and confident. He still had the occasional bout of self-doubt, but he no longer felt like a complete imposter in this strange new world, with its foreign customs and language and attitudes.

At least not all the time. "Yo, Stubbs," a guy from his hall named Hunter called out as Dexter headed back to his dorm room one Saturday morning after a study session at the library. "Been looking for you, man. Want to check out my new ride? Birthday gift from dear old Dad—just dropped it off this morning."

"Without a doubt." Dexter grinned, swallowing back a pang of envy. Despite his best efforts, he couldn't completely avoid occasional reminders that he was very different from most of the people there. But as long as *they* didn't know that, what difference did those differences make? "But can I take a rain check? I'm supposed to meet Daisy downstairs in five."

"No problem, dude." Hunter waggled his eyebrows suggestively. "You definitely don't want to keep a girl like that waiting."

Dexter grinned, a flush of pride drowning out the envy over Hunter's new car. Who needed a Mercedes or a BMW when he had Daisy? "You know it, brother. Catch you later."

He ducked into his room to drop off his books, noticing as he did that the little red light on his answering machine was flashing insistently. *Probably just Mom or Aunt Paula calling again,* he told himself with a grimace. He'd been avoiding most of their calls, which seemed more and more frequent lately. He knew he would have to talk to them sooner or later, but it just seemed too soon to let his old life intrude on his new one.

Ignoring the message, he let himself out of the room and hurried down the hall. Bypassing the elevator, he headed into the echoing stairwell of the high-rise dorm, taking the steps three at a time. Sometimes it was hard to believe how well almost everything was going so far. It was as if he feared he might wake up, the dream shattered by the insistent whine of the alarm clock in his tiny bedroom back home.

Back home where you belong, boy. His aunt's voice, nasty and harsh as ever, burst into his head so clearly that it was as if she were right there in the stairwell with him.

Dexter shook his head impatiently, like a horse shaking off a pesky fly. The more time passed, the more he was realizing just how badly his aunt had treated him all his life. Not only had she considered him her own personal slave, but she'd all but told him he didn't deserve any better.

Then there was his mother. He knew she loved him and meant well, but how could she hope to offer him hope for the future when she was so hopeless and downtrodden herself? Together, the two women had spent a lifetime making Dexter think he didn't deserve anything better than what he had. The saddest part was how completely he'd believed it.

But that was the old Dexter, he told himself firmly as he reached the bottom of the steps. *The new Dexter knows better. All I have to do is remember that.*

Daisy was waiting in the dorm lobby, dressed in pink-and-white-striped pants and a sleeveless white blouse that showed off her slim, tanned arms. "Hey, cutie," she greeted him, tilting back her head for his kiss. "Ready to go? I'm famished."

Two hours later, after a leisurely lunch at an off-campus eatery, Dexter and Daisy strolled across the college green hand in hand, enjoying each other's company and the warmth of the Indian-summer day. As usual, the green was filled with students sunning themselves, tossing Frisbees or kicking soccer balls, napping in the shade, making out, holding debates, strumming acoustic guitars, reading magazines, studying. Going about their lives.

I'm one of them now, Dexter thought with a shiver of new-Dexter happiness tinged with just a touch of old-Dexter disbelief. *Nobody looking at me would ever know otherwise.*

For a moment he was almost overwhelmed by a feeling of contentment and well-being. This was where he was meant to be. Maybe all his life he'd known that in some subconscious way. Maybe that was why he'd never bothered to rebel against his lot in life, to fight back with drugs or aggression or petty crime like so many young men in his situation. His aunt had always said it was because he was a natural-born wimp, but that wasn't it at all. It was because he knew something better was coming if only he was patient.

As he glanced around again at the idyllic scene, Dexter suddenly noticed something new in the midst of it—a familiar, lumbering shape making its way down the sidewalk just a short distance away across the nearest patch of lawn. It was as if an enormous, bulging black cloud had just blocked out the sun's warmth, sending a chill over the whole campus.

No, Dexter thought, his stomach lurching and roiling with shock. *No, no, no, no, no!*

"Hey! What's the matter?" Daisy yanked her hand out of his grip and rubbed it with her free hand. "You just about squeezed my fingers off!"

"S-sorry," Dexter stammered, his mind a howling whirlwind of panic as he stared at his aunt just a few dozen yards away, big as life. His mother was there, too, standing like a meek shadow of the larger woman. He couldn't let his two worlds, the two Dexters, collide—it would ruin everything. If Daisy ever met his mother and aunt, it would blow his cover. She would know immediately that he'd been lying to her about his happy, wealthy, tight-knit family; that his stories about the laughter-filled nightly dinners and the leisurely vacations in Europe and all the rest were lies. It would be a disaster.

Frozen with terror, he watched Aunt Paula accost a passing coed while his mother hung back timidly, her hands clutching her pocketbook as if she feared someone might snatch it away at any moment. Dexter was too far away to hear what Aunt Paula was saying, but after a moment he saw the coed shrug and move on, leaving the two women standing there staring around uncertainly. They couldn't have looked more out of place if they'd suddenly showed up on Mars—his mother with her thin, hunched shoulders and careworn face, and Aunt Paula looking like the world's fattest drag queen in one of the tacky outfits she'd bought with her winnings.

They don't belong here, he thought frantically. *Why are they here?*

But he quickly realized that it didn't matter. Whatever they were doing there, he was going to have to do something about it—*now*—if he didn't want to see his carefully constructed new life come crashing down around him.

"Hey, listen," Dexter said to Daisy, desperately trying to sound casual. "I just remembered I, uh, promised to call my cousin in Switzerland. Birthday—it's her birthday today. I'd better go do it before it gets too late over there. Do you mind if we meet up a little later?"

If Daisy noticed the slightly hysterical squeak that crept into his voice on the last few words, she didn't show it. "Wait a minute. What cousin in Switzerland? Are you trying to ditch me?" she demanded with a playful pout.

He forced a laugh. "Now why would I want to ditch the most beautiful girl in the world?" he asked, the familiar compliment rolling easily off his tongue. "I'll make it up to you— how about dinner tonight? Anywhere you want. My treat."

Her pout turned into a smile. "Well, when you put it that way . . ." she said. "I guess I can live without you for a little while. My roommate wanted to go downtown for some shopping anyway. Maybe I can find something sexy to wear for our dinner tonight." She winked. "Tell your cousin I said happy birthday."

With a little wave, she turned and strolled off in the direction of her own dorm. Normally he would have happily watched her walk away all day, but at the moment he was too anxious and impatient to enjoy the view. When she finally disappeared from sight, he let out a sigh of relief.

And not a moment too soon . . .

"Dexter!" his aunt bellowed, her voice like a foghorn cutting through the clamor of the chatting, laughing, music-playing students. "There you are, boy!"

"What luck!" His mother's much quieter voice quavered with relief as the two women hurried toward him.

Dexter did his best to scan the surrounding area out of the corner of his eye as they approached. Was that girl sitting under the tree over there shooting him a funny look? Did he recognize those guys over by the fountain from his Spanish class? Who was out there watching what he was doing, just waiting to give everyone he knew a full report on his embarrassing relatives?

Luckily he was pretty sure he didn't see anyone he actually knew. Deciding not to take any chances, he grabbed his mother firmly by the elbow as she reached out for a hug. "Come this way, Mom," he said. "Let's go somewhere quiet to talk."

"Surprised to see us?" Aunt Paula demanded, not budging as he tried to maneuver around her.

"Surprised . . . surprised doesn't even cover it." Dexter went for a joking tone and failed miserably. "Come on, really. Let's get out of the sun so we can chat."

He managed to steer them around the corner of the main library to a deserted patch of grass and ferns beneath the shade of an ancient, gnarled maple tree between buildings. Dropping his mother's arm, he turned to face them.

"So what are you guys doing here?" he demanded. "Why didn't you let me know you were coming?"

"We tried." Aunt Paula sounded peeved. "If you ever answered your damn phone . . ."

"Never mind." Dexter's mother made tentative soothing motions with her hands. "We're here together now, and that's what matters." She turned her pale eyes onto Dexter. "I've missed you, Dexy. Why haven't you come home to visit? Or at least called?"

Dexter felt a hollow ache in his heart at the desperate need in her face. "It's only been a few weeks," he protested weakly. "I've been settling in and stuff . . . you know, busy."

"That's right. You're some big important college boy now, too busy for family." Aunt Paula snorted. "Good thing I wasn't too busy for family the day I wrote out that fat check to this place."

"Paula, please." Dexter's mother's eyes pleaded with her. "Let's not fight. I want to hear all about what Dexy has been doing up here. Are you making any friends in this place?" Once again her anxious gaze fixed on his face.

"Sure, Mom. Everyone here is really cool." Dexter hadn't felt comfortable discussing his social life when he was an outcast back in high school, and he found it wasn't any more pleasant now that he actually had friends.

"Any girlfriends?" Aunt Paula joked. "Sowing your wild oats now that you're out of your mother's house, Dexy?"

Dexter shrugged, feeling himself blush. "I dunno . . ." he mumbled.

"Leave him alone, Paula." His mother looked almost as embarrassed as he felt at the topic. "Now Dexter, what about your classes? Did you declare your major yet?"

"Yeah, what's it going to be, boy?" Aunt Paula demanded. "Pre-med, like we talked about, right? Huh?"

Dexter almost wished they could go back to discussing his social life. "Um, I signed up for most of the stuff you said," he said. "Biology, Chemistry, Economics. And Spanish, for the language requirement. Oh, and one elective—British Literature." He mumbled the final two words as quietly as possible.

"British Literature?" Aunt Paula pursed her fleshy lips disapprovingly. "Why'd you go and sign up for something like that?"

"I just thought it sounded interesting." Dexter hated feeling on the defensive against his overbearing aunt. It was why he'd spent most of his life doing whatever she said.

She scowled. "Don't take that tone with me, boy. This ain't a joke—a fruity class like that could really mess up your grades, keep you from getting into medical school someday."

"Don't worry. I already got one paper back, and I got an A."

Dexter didn't bother to add that it was by far the best grade he'd received in any class so far that semester. The truth was, even after only a few weeks he was already struggling in most of his other classes. His mind didn't seem to want to grasp the complexities of chemistry or biology, and economics was just plain dull.

"Anyway," he added quickly, before they could think to ask about the rest of his grades, "British Lit isn't necessarily as impractical as you think. From what I hear, college liberal arts professors make decent money, and—"

"Forget about that right this minute, boy," Aunt Paula cut him off harshly. "I'm not shelling out all my hard-earned money for my nephew to go off and become some tweedy, snooty professor type."

Dexter recoiled as if she'd slapped him. Why had he bothered? Better to stick to the script, telling his family only as much as they needed to know and keeping the rest to himself.

Of course, he wouldn't be able to hide certain things from

them forever. What would his mother and Aunt Paula say when they saw his grades at the end of the term?

For a moment all the lies and half-truths he was telling crowded into his mind, making him feel dizzy and sick. What was he trying to do, anyway? Did he real think this whole two-Dexters thing could last?

But he quickly pushed such worries aside. Where there was a will, there was a way. Maybe he could bring his grades up before the end of the semester if he worked harder, sought out extra tutoring, whatever. The most important thing was to keep himself there at school. Now that the life of his dreams seemed almost within his grasp, there was no way he was giving it up. No matter what it took.

11

"THIS PLACE SUCKS." SHANNON scowled down at the half-eaten bag of pretzels in her hand. "If things keep on like this, we're all going to starve to death before the stupid rescuers get here."

Dexter glanced up from his own chunk of stale airline roll and smiled sympathetically. He had to admit that it wasn't much of a lunch. As soon as the drenching rain had ended a few minutes earlier, the three of them had realized they were hungry and gone in search of food, only to find that the rationing had already started in earnest.

Boone sighed loudly and shot his sister an irritated look. "Yeah, we know, Shannon. Instead of complaining, why don't you do something about it?" he challenged.

"Like what?" She put her hands on her hips and glared at him. "Call for a pizza?"

"Maybe we could go out and look for more food sources,"

Dexter put in mildly, trying to keep the peace. "I heard there are lots of fruit trees not far from the beach, but they're already getting picked clean. We could look for some new trees farther in. Or a freshwater source, maybe."

Boone shrugged. "Sounds like a plan to me." He glanced at Shannon. "You in? Or would you rather stick around here and work on your tan as usual?"

"Get over yourself, you—"

"Hi, guys," a new, British-accented voice said, interrupting. "What's going on?"

Dexter glanced up to see a young, bearded man wandering up to them with Arzt trailing along behind. He had seen the bearded British guy around the beach—he'd been part of the transceiver group along with Shannon and Boone, for one thing—but so far he hadn't actually met him. At the moment he looked kind of bored. Dexter wondered if Arzt had been lecturing him on science or something.

"Hi," Dexter said to the British guy. "I don't think we've met. I'm Dexter."

"Charlie," the newcomer offered his hand. "Nice to meet you, Dexter."

Meanwhile Arzt flopped onto the sand, panting and sweating. "Geez," he complained. "First that rain, now this heat—this place is like a freaking sauna."

"Charlie used to be in that band, Driveshaft," Shannon told Dexter lazily, ignoring Arzt's comment. "I'm sure he'll tell you all about it if you want."

Charlie looked slightly pained. "Not used to," he corrected. "*Am*. We never really broke up. Not officially."

"Driveshaft? I remember them." Dexter was impressed. "Cool."

Boone seemed less interested in the whole conversation. "We were just talking about going into the jungle to look for more fruit and freshwater," he told the two newcomers. "Want to come along?"

Charlie glanced toward the jungle, a shadow of apprehension crossing his face. But then he shrugged. "Sure," he said. "I guess so."

"I'll come, too." Arzt climbed to his feet and stretched. "Won't do you any good to look for food sources without someone who knows what they're looking for."

"And you do?" Charlie cocked one eyebrow skeptically.

Arzt shrugged. "I'm a man of science, my boy," he said with a slightly haughty air.

As the others started talking about which direction to go, Dexter noticed the tall, auburn-haired woman from the transceiver group walking in their direction, her head down and her expression troubled. Someone on his work team had mentioned that her name was Kate and that she seemed to be friends with Jack. Dexter watched her as she wandered closer, wondering why she looked so upset.

"Hi," he called to her, deciding to take his role as the island's amateur psychologist into his own hands. "It's Kate, right?"

She glanced up, startled. "Yeah."

Dexter introduced himself, though most of the others seemed to know her already. "We're heading into the jungle on a food search," he said. "Interested?"

"Sure, I'll come along." Kate stepped toward them, sweeping a lock of her curly hair out of her eyes. "I could stand to get away from this beach for a while."

Dexter noticed that as she said it, her gaze wandered briefly to the blue-and-yellow infirmary tent. Drifting out from inside were an increasing number of distressing groans and cries of pain. He'd heard that the man inside, the one who'd had that big chunk of shrapnel stuck in his side, was probably dying despite Jack's best efforts.

He shuddered and turned away, not wanting to think about that too much. "Great," he told Kate. "The more the merrier."

Soon all six of them were heading toward the tree line. As they neared it, they passed Walt, who was kicking at the sand in the shade of a palm tree.

Dexter paused, surprised to see him out there alone. So far Walt always seemed to be with either his father or the inscrutable John Locke, with whom he seemed to have struck up a friendship. But neither man was in sight at the moment.

"Hey," Dexter greeted the boy. "What are you up to, Walt? Where's your dad?"

Walt squinted up at him. "In the jungle looking for Vincent."

"Vincent?" Dexter felt a pang. In all his worry over Daisy, he hadn't bothered to consider that other survivors still might be searching for loved ones as well. "Is that your brother?"

"No." Walt gave him an are-you-crazy look. "My dog."

"Oh." Dexter belatedly recalled that the boy had mentioned his missing dog before. "Well, I hope he finds him."

Leaving the boy to his sand-kicking, he and the others continued their trek. Soon they were making their way along an animal trail in the dappled shade of the swaying palms. It was much cooler in there, and Dexter was relieved to escape the scorching heat of the beach. As Arzt had mentioned, the recent rain had failed to cool things off, instead merely raising the humidity and making the afternoon sun feel even hotter. In such conditions it sometimes seemed impossible to drink enough water to avoid getting overheated and dehydrated, and Dexter didn't want to take any chances. He was already having enough problems with hallucinations and weird memory gaps.

After a few minutes the trail narrowed, becoming a tiny track through a large, boulder-studded section of the forest. The hikers were forced to move along two by two. Dexter fell into step beside Shannon at the end of the line. Her pretty face wore a grumpy expression, and sweat dotted her forehead and dampened her blond hair.

"Remind me *not* to book my next vacation anywhere with stupid palm trees. This tropical weather is way overrated," she grumbled, kicking aside a palm frond lying in her way.

Dexter smiled sympathetically. "You sound like Daisy," he said. "She'd pick a ski trip in Vail over a beach vacation in the islands any day of the week."

"I used to love the beach." Shannon wrinkled her nose. "But these days it's getting a little old, you know?"

"Yeah. Hold on a sec." Dexter had just spotted a puddle of clear water in the cleft of a nearby boulder. Even in the relative cool of the jungle shade, the heat was oppressive enough to arouse his thirst. "That looks like rainwater—think I'll grab a quick drink."

Shannon wrinkled her nose. "Are you sure it's safe?"

"Guess we'll find out." Dexter grinned, then pushed his way through the tall grass toward the boulder. The others were a dozen yards ahead and didn't seem to notice, but Shannon stopped and waited for him.

He stepped carefully over to the boulder, then leaned down to drink. The puddle lay in a shaft of sunlight shooting down between the trees, which made white flashes dance on its placid surface.

As his face and hands neared it, preparing to scoop it up, the glassy water caught Dexter's reflection in its surface. His face seemed to shimmer and shift—the familiar eyes looking up at him suddenly went dark, angry, and alien, and the corners of his mouth turned down into a scowl . . .

"Yow!" he shouted, so startled that he jumped backward and nearly tripped over a fallen branch behind him.

"What?" Shannon cried. "What's wrong, Dexter?"

He stared at the water, which was still and glassy again, showing only his ordinary face. "My reflection," he said slowly. "It—it changed. Like there was someone else in there looking back at me."

She frowned. "What are you talking about? Don't scare me like that—I thought you stepped on a snake or something."

"But I saw it," he insisted, too spooked by what he'd just seen to worry about what she might think. "I swear. I was looking at my own face, and it just . . . changed." When the words came out of his mouth, they sounded weak even to him.

Shannon glanced toward the puddle, looking unconvinced and a little impatient. "Don't freak out. It was probably just rainwater dripping down from the trees up there." She gestured to the jungle canopy overhead. "It could've rippled the water and caused an optical illusion that made you think your face looked different—like those fun-house mirrors that make people look fat or whatever."

"You're probably right," Dexter said slowly, still unable to shake the memory of that furious face—his own, and yet not his own—glaring up at him. "But . . ."

"But what?" she asked distractedly, glancing in the direction of the others, whose voices had faded almost out of earshot. "Come on, we'd better catch up with those guys. I don't want to get lost in here."

Dexter followed as she headed up the path. But he was still thinking about what he'd just seen. "You know, this isn't the first weird thing I've seen around this place since the crash . . ." Hoping she wouldn't think he was crazy—at least any more than she already did—he told her about spotting his doppelganger in the jungle the day before.

"Jack said you were pretty badly dehydrated after the crash, right?" she said when he'd finished. "Couldn't that be making your mind play tricks on you?"

"Sure," he admitted. "I guess it could. But the reason I went out there looking was because a couple of other people thought they saw me in places where I hadn't been." He shook his head. "I know it sounds crazy. But anyway, even if it was just a trick of my mind, why would it be making me see *that*? What does it mean?"

Shannon shrugged, not looking very interested. "I don't know." She shot him a playful smirk. "Sounds like a question for Dr. Dexter Cross, Boy Psychologist."

"I guess." Dexter wasn't sure why, but her words caused a knot of anxiety in the pit of his stomach. At that moment they rounded a bend in the trail. The others were just ahead, gathered at the base of a tree, staring up into its branches. "Come on, let's go see what those guys found."

12

DEXTER'S STOMACH CHURNED WITH anxiety as he glanced up at the calendar hanging over the desk in his tiny dorm room. It was already December, which meant only a couple of weeks remained before winter break. He'd had enough reason to dread it already, knowing he would have to return home and face his family. But he also had a couple of other reasons to look forward to the end of the semester with anxiety.

Quit obsessing about it, he scolded himself, glancing down at the open books on his desk and then at the blinking computer screen in front of him. *At least until you finish your paper, anyway. It's bad enough you're probably going to flunk three out of your five classes as it is; you don't have to sabotage what should be your best grade this semester. . . .*

He sighed, his mind wandering despite his best intentions. Glancing at the stack of thick, intimidating-looking science and Econ books stacked on the floor beside the desk, he shuddered. It would take the next best thing to a miracle for him to pass those three difficult classes, let alone do well in them. No matter how hard he studied, he just couldn't seem to get the hang of chemistry or biology. And economics simply bored him so much that he couldn't seem to retain the information in the books or the professor's lectures.

Dexter's door was ajar to take advantage of his neighbor's stereo, which was blasting rap music. It seemed Dexter was the only one on the hall who didn't have a top-of-the-line sound system, along with a TV and DVD player and various other fancy appliances. A few of the guys had commented on Dexter's spare, gadget-free room, but he had managed to deflect their curiosity with a convoluted story about his imaginary mother's new beliefs in Buddhism and minimalism. To his surprise, they seemed to have bought it.

And why shouldn't they? he thought with a by-now-familiar flash of guilt. *They have no reason to think I'd lie to them.*

As he forced his eyes back to his computer screen, he heard the door squeak open a little farther. He glanced up, expecting to see one of the guys from the hall stopping by to invite him out for a drink or to watch the game. Instead, Daisy's smiling blond head poked in.

"Knock knock!" she sang out. "Surprise! I was just passing your building, so I figured I'd pop in."

"Hey!" Quickly pushing aside his worries, he sprang to his feet and hurried over to her. Somehow, just seeing her face usually made all his problems seem a little less daunting. He would work it all out—after all, he had no choice. He leaned down to give her a kiss, then kicked aside some dirty clothes, notebooks, and crumpled food wrappers that were littering the carpet. "Come on in. Sorry the place is a mess."

She waved aside the familiar apology, following him back over to his desk. "So I'm supposed to meet Cara in a while—we're going to Forty-Two for dinner. Want to come along?" She grinned at him hopefully.

Dexter's stomach gave an extra twist. Forty-Two was one of the most expensive restaurants in town—one of Daisy's favorite spots for an impromptu meal. Far too much of Aunt Paula's money, along with that from Dexter's part-time job at the bursar's office, had disappeared into the restaurant's till.

That was another problem he was trying not to think about. So far he'd managed to maintain his charade as a rich kid who only worked part-time on campus because his fictional wealthy parents thought it would "build character." But that charade would come to an end if—or, rather, *when*—he ran out of money. It was turning out to be more expensive than he ever could have imagined, this business of having a girlfriend who was accustomed to the very best. How was he going to keep it up if the funds Aunt Paula had allotted him for the semester ran out before winter break? He'd heard of people selling their blood for extra cash—more and more often lately, he found himself wondering uneasily just exactly how that worked.

"So how about it?" Daisy wheedled. "Can you take a break from your paper for a while?"

That reminded him that he had the perfect excuse to avoid this one expensive dinner, at least. "Sorry," he said. "I really need to crank this thing out—I'm going to need to start studying for my econ final this week if I want to pass. Rain check?"

"Okay." She seemed only mildly disappointed by the brush-off. Leaning over his shoulder, she peered at words on the computer screen. "So how's the paper going? You decided to do Dickens, right?"

"Yeah. It's going okay. How about your Chaucer paper?"

"Almost finished. That's why I'm going out to celebrate." She winked playfully. "That reminds me—when are you going to know your plans for the break? I can't wait for you to meet my family. And you'll love the beach house. It sounds a lot like your uncle's place in Cabo."

Dexter's stomach lurched once again. Daisy had been talking more and more lately about the two of them hanging out together during the break—preferably with her family at their oceanfront Florida vacation home. So far he'd been putting off the issue, claiming that he had to check in with his own family before committing to anything, but he knew he would have to give her an answer before much longer. She clearly expected him to spend at least part of the break with her, but he knew that his mother and aunt were expecting to have him home with them the whole time. How was he going to keep his two worlds separate this time?

Feeling desperate, he decided it was time to address it before things got any more out of hand. "I meant to call you about that," he said slowly, the lies forming in his mind as he spoke them. "I think that's going to have to be another rain check."

"What do you mean?" This time she looked genuinely crestfallen.

"I talked to my folks today," he said, trying not to feel guilty about deceiving her. It wasn't easy, not with those guileless blue eyes gazing at him so trustingly. But with effort, he swallowed back the urge to fall at her feet and confess everything. "They really want me to spend this break doing volunteer work with the poor in—in Spain." The last part was inspired by a quick glance at his Spanish language textbook, as he was trying to think of a spot appropriately distant from Florida. "It's sort of a family tradition," he went on quickly. "My father did it when he was a student, and his father before him. Just our way of giving back a little, you know? Like public service or whatever. So now it's my turn."

"Oh." She fell silent for a moment, obviously digesting what he'd just said. "I guess that sounds kind of cool. It's a really nice tradition, actually. And it should be a great experience for you—it'd be selfish of me to complain, right?" She smiled wanly. "I'll miss you like crazy, though. When are you getting back from overseas?"

"I'm not sure yet. I'll be back in plenty of time for next semester, though." He held his breath, hardly daring to believe that she'd bought his spur-of-the-moment excuse.

"Good. Will you promise me one thing? Will you come back to campus a day early? My parents are going to drive me back, so that way at least you can meet them."

Dexter hesitated only a second before nodding. "Of course," he said, touched that she cared so much. "I promise."

"Good." She was all smiles again. Glancing at her watch, she let out a little gasp. "Oops! I'm late—Cara is going to kill me." She bent down to plant a kiss on his forehead. "Don't get up—I'm out of here."

"Have fun. I'll call you later."

He watched as she skipped out the door and disappeared. Even though some of the complications were giving him ulcers, he hardly dared to believe how much his life had improved in the past few months. Here he was at one of the best universities in the country with the most amazing girlfriend in the world begging to spend more time with him.

Lucky. Lucky, lucky me, he thought.

He ran a finger lightly over his scar, hoping he wouldn't regret his promise about meeting her parents. How was he going to explain that one to his mother and Aunt Paula? Still, he didn't worry about it too much. He would come up with something. So far he always had.

Maybe my luck really has changed, he thought, his paper forgotten as he gazed at the ceiling, contemplating his own change of fortune. *I mean, you hear all the time about formerly successful people who fall on hard times through bad decisions or bad luck. Why shouldn't the opposite happen sometimes too? After all, isn't it my turn?*

13

"DUDES!" HURLEY SAID APPRECIATIVELY, grabbing a piece of fresh fruit out of the pile Boone had just dumped on the sand. "This is awesome! Where'd you find this stuff?"

"Out that way . . ." Kate pointed and, with Charlie's and Boone's help, started describing where they'd found the fruit as more castaways gathered around to exclaim over it.

Dexter wasn't really paying attention, though. After dumping his share of the load and stretching his shoulders, he wandered away from the group. Finding the fruit trees had distracted him from his own problems, but now that he was back on the beach he couldn't seem to stop glancing over at the fuselage. He knew that he wouldn't be able to put his mind at rest until he checked in there for Daisy.

A sudden yelp of pain emerged from the infirmary tent, distracting him. The injured man's cries and groans seemed to be getting worse rather than better. Dexter glanced over that way as he wandered toward one of the rainwater-collection tubs for a drink. He noticed that many of his fellow castaways were also staring in that direction, most of them grimacing or looking upset.

Just then, Jack stepped out of the tent and hurried toward the water tub. The doctor, who looked weary and bedraggled, was holding several empty plastic cups made out of old water bottles.

"How's it going in there?" Dexter asked when Jack reached the tub.

Jack bent over and scooped up some water. Then he straightened and glanced back toward the tent before meeting Dexter's eye.

"Could be better," he said, his voice sounding a bit strained. "But we're not giving up yet." He hurried off with his water before Dexter could answer.

Most of the others were still busy with the fruit. Once he finished drinking, Dexter wandered down the beach, trying to distract himself from his guilty thoughts about checking the fuselage. He noticed a lone figure sitting a short distance away and headed over to see who it was. When he got a little closer, he recognized Locke.

Dexter hesitated, staring at the back of the older man's balding head. There was something about John Locke that made him a little uneasy. Maybe it was the way the man's pale blue eyes seemed to see more than they should about people. Then again, maybe it was just because he was a little odd, keeping to himself and talking mostly to young Walt. Either way, Dexter almost turned away again. Then, out of the corner of his eye, he caught a glimpse of the fuselage looming behind him. That made him set his jaw and step forward, not wanting to let one more thing about this island scare him.

"Hi there," Dexter said, stepping around in front of Locke and lifting a hand in greeting. "I just wanted to let you know a bunch of us found a few new fruit trees not too far from here. We brought a bunch of fruit back—there's plenty over there if you want some."

Locke was sitting on a makeshift bench amidst the wreckage carving at a sliver of wood with a small knife. For a moment Dexter thought the other man wasn't going to answer at all. Locke merely glanced up at him before returning his attention to his work.

Finally, though, he spoke. "No thanks." His voice was surprisingly soft and cultured. "Not hungry."

Emboldened by the response, however grudging, Dexter spoke again. "What's that you're carving?" he asked curiously.

"Whistle."

"Cool." Dexter thought it was sort of an odd project, but he supposed it was no worse a way to pass the time than any other. "Looks like you know what you're doing. Do you think it will work when you're done?"

Locke glanced up at him, squinting against the rays of the sun, which had crested the firmament some hours earlier and was now sinking slowly back down toward the ocean. "Oh, it will work," he assured Dexter with quiet confidence. "The only question is, what's going to show up when I blow it?"

The other man's pale blue eyes, the right one bisected by a painful-looking cut, were starting to give Dexter the creeps. For one crazy second he felt as though Locke might be looking right through his eyes and into his heart and mind, maybe even seeing something Dexter couldn't see himself.

"Well, guess I'd better let other people know about the fruit," he said, shaking off the eerie feeling. "Good luck with that whistle."

On his way back up the beach he passed Charlie, who was once again wandering around looking slightly bored. Dexter nodded but didn't stop to chat. Suddenly he felt the need to be alone for a while.

Once he was a short distance away from camp he drifted down to the surf's edge. Kicking off his shoes, he strolled along toward the south, enjoying the cool feel of the wet sand beneath his feet. For a few minutes he was able to forget about the confusion and anxiety of the past couple of days and just enjoy the natural beauty of his surroundings.

Of course, it would be a lot nicer if Daisy were here to enjoy it with me . . .

That thought jarred him back to reality. He paused and glanced back toward the wreckage-strewn beach, his eyes drawn immediately toward the crash's horrific centerpiece— the fuselage. As usual, he felt a mixture of cowardice and guilt when he imagined Daisy's lifeless body still strapped into one of the seats inside. Why couldn't he just go in there and face whatever he might find?

He was distracted by the sound of people talking somewhere just ahead. First he heard the sound of a woman's voice, agitated yet quiet. Then a louder, angrier male voice answered her, though Dexter couldn't make out what either of the arguers was saying.

He took a few more steps down the beach and around some boulders, bringing him within sight of a rocky little cove just around a bend in the shoreline. Then he realized why he couldn't understand the voices. Standing there facing each other, so far unaware of his presence, were the Asian man who'd offered him that slimy-looking raw seafood on his first waking day, along with the pretty Asian woman everyone assumed was his wife. Someone had told Dexter that the pair was Korean and that neither one of them spoke a word of English; as far as Dexter knew, nobody even knew their names. They kept to themselves most of the time, though the man occasionally wandered around offering up his repulsive-looking seafood. Some of the survivors actually seemed to enjoy his island version of sushi, though Dexter still couldn't bring himself to try it.

Dexter winced as the man let out a frustrated shout. The woman refused to shout back, instead turning away. The expression on her face was a mixture of bitterness and anguished disappointment. Seeing it made Dexter's stomach clench in an uncomfortable way.

That's exactly how Daisy looked.

The memory popped into his head as if it had always been there, though a moment ago he hadn't been aware of its existence. Now, though, he quite clearly recalled looking into his girlfriend's face as she turned away from him with that same anguished expression.

But why? He searched his mind for the answer, but there seemed to be a black hole where the rest of the memory should have been. He had no idea whether they had merely bickered over something stupid, the way Boone and Shannon did all day long, or fought about a more serious matter.

Daisy and I don't bicker, he thought. Despite his newly discovered memory holes, he knew that much was true.

The thought wasn't particularly comforting, though. If they hadn't been bickering, the fight must have been over something serious. So why couldn't he remember it?

He turned and wandered back toward the main part of the beach. As he walked, he did his best to focus on that image of Daisy's angry, disappointed face. It might be painful, but it seemed to be his only clue, his only chance of finding answers to his questions.

"Hey, man. Where'd you run off to just now?"

Glancing up, Dexter saw that he'd almost walked straight into Boone, who was at the water's edge rinsing off his hands in the surf. "Hey," he greeted him. "I just went to get a drink."

Boone straightened up and peered at him. "You all right?" he asked. "You look kind of—I don't know. Weird."

"Thanks a lot, dude." Dexter smiled weakly, then sighed. "Yeah, but you're right. I'm feeling kind of weird, too."

"Do you need more water?" Boone asked with concern. "I could run up and get you some, or—"

"No, it's not that." For a moment Dexter was ready to brush him off with a shallow excuse. Then he realized Boone was probably the closest thing he had to a friend on this island. Maybe talking to someone would make him feel better. Wasn't that how it was supposed to work? Dexter glanced down and poked at the damp sand with his toe, trying to figure out how to explain. "I'm just kind of feeling like a loser because I'm too chicken to go into the fuselage and check for Daisy." He shrugged awkwardly. "For all I know she could have been rotting away in there since the crash while I was out looking for her in the jungle or wherever."

Boone stared at him, his blue eyes uncertain. "You don't sound that upset about it, man," he said, his voice verging on accusatory. "Come to think of it, you haven't really seemed all *that* worried about finding your girlfriend this whole time. I noticed from the start, but figured it was just the dehydration working you over, so I cut you some slack . . ."

"Yeah, I know." As soon as he heard the words come out of the other guy's mouth, Dexter realized they were true. This whole time, it was almost as if finding Daisy were an afterthought—something he constantly had to remind himself about. And there was a reason for that. The truth had just slid into place in his head, another memory out of nowhere. "See, I'm not even sure if Daisy was on the plane."

"What?" Boone looked startled. "But I thought you said—"

"She was booked on the flight," Dexter explained, wondering why he was just remembering this now. "But we had a big fight right before we left Sydney and so I didn't see her when we boarded. She might have switched flights or just switched seats. I don't really know."

"That's rough, man." Boone gazed at him curiously.

Dexter could tell he was wondering what they had fought about. The trouble was, he was still wondering that himself. As clear as that image was of Daisy's angry face, he couldn't quite move beyond it to the details of what had caused it.

The hole in his memory disturbed him, making him feel off-kilter and not quite himself. "You know, I just realized what I need to do," he told Boone firmly, not allowing himself to second-guess the impulse that had just grabbed him. "I've got to go check in the fuselage—right now, before it gets too dark. At least that way I'll know, one way or the other."

"Okay." Boone gazed at him, still looking curious and uncertain. "Good luck with that."

Dexter thanked him and hurried off toward the fuselage, not giving himself a chance to back down. The sky over the beach was fading to pink with the sunset, the beauty of the lush tropical island out of sync with the scattered refuse of the crash and the horrific groans of the injured man in the infirmary tent.

But Dexter hardly noticed any of it. Pausing only long enough to find a flashlight in a handy pile of supplies, he headed straight toward his goal. The fuselage filled his eyes and mind as he approached it. He drifted to a stop a few yards from the dark, jagged opening, staring up into the blackness. All his fears crowded back as he heard the buzz of the flies from inside and caught a whiff of the stench.

Taking a deep breath, he gathered his courage and stepped forward. He knew what he needed to do; now all that was left was to do it. . . .

14

"DO YOU SEE THAT?" Aunt Paula threw up her hands in disgust, making the gaudy gold bracelets she wore everywhere these days jangle loudly against one another. She glared at the tiny figures taking part in the TV crime drama. "That detective guy better clear outta the way and let the doctors do their thing, or that girl will never live to tell him who killed those eight people."

"The emergency room always looks so exciting. Maybe Dexy will wind up working there when he's a doctor." Dexter's mother turned around in her seat on the new leather sofa and smiled at him.

Dexter drew in a deep breath, trying to work up the courage to do what he knew he needed to do. The winter break was almost over, and he still hadn't found the opportunity to talk to the two women about heading back to school early, let alone broken the news to them about his grades.

Now or never, he told himself.

"Never" sounded like a tempting option. But he ignored the temptation, adding his half-empty cereal bowl to the sink full of dirty dishes and walking out of the kitchen alcove to join the two women in the tiny living room. After all, why shouldn't this work out just like everything else had been working out for him lately? If his luck truly had changed, he had nothing to fear from telling the truth.

Besides, maybe wasn't giving his mother and aunt enough credit. Once upon a time he couldn't have imagined them encouraging him to go to college at all. If he simply explained things to them, perhaps they would see that he needed to follow his own path when it came to choosing a major. The thought made him feel a little better, and he cleared his throat.

"Listen," he spoke up firmly. "I've been meaning to talk to you guys about something."

For a second the women seemed disinclined to turn away from the TV program. But finally his mother seemed to notice something different in his voice and turned to gaze at him quizzically.

"What is it, Dexy?" she asked.

"It's about my major."

This time Aunt Paula, too, turned away from the TV. "What about it?" she said. "Did you declare Pre-med yet, or what? You better get off your butt about it if you want to get into a good med school someday."

"But that's just it," Dexter said. "I—I don't think I want to go to medical school. I don't really think I could even if I did want to. See, my grades . . . Well, they weren't so hot this term. At least not in my science classes."

"What?" His mother's eyes widened. "But Dexy, I thought you told us you were doing just fine! What happened?"

"I did do fine in English," Dexter said, feeling a slight swell of pride as he remembered his professor's encouraging comments on his final paper. "Great, actually. Got an A minus. I did okay in Spanish and even Econ, too—B in Spanish, C plus in Econ."

"What about your science classes?" Aunt Paula demanded. "Those are the important ones for your Pre-med, you know."

"I know. But I just couldn't pull them off, I guess." He shrugged weakly, almost afraid to mention the actual grades. "Uh, I think I ended up with a D in Bio, and D minus in Chem. Sorry."

His mother looked horrified. "Oh, Dexy . . ." she whispered.

"How'd you manage to screw up so bad, boy?" Aunt Paula snapped. "You never got grades that crappy in high school, didja? Otherwise they wouldn'ta let you into that fancy college in the first place."

"I know." Dexter tried to keep the whiny defensiveness out of his voice. Any hint of weakness, and Aunt Paula would attack like a shark. "But college courses are a lot more challenging. And like I'm trying to tell you, I just don't think I have much aptitude for the whole science thing."

He expected Aunt Paula to berate him for being lazy or stupid. Instead she sat there for a moment looking thoughtful. Then she glanced at his mother and gave a quick shrug.

"Sounds like our boy ain't cut out for the doctoring thing," she said. "Guess we shoulda seen that coming, after the way he cried like a baby when he cut up his face that time."

Dexter winced, resisting the urge to reach up and rub his scar as both women turned to stare at it. Why did his aunt always have to bring up that embarrassing old story? He still remembered it as if it had happened yesterday. Fourth grade; the usual bullies. Pushed over the edge by their usual taunts—about his looks, his clothes, his lack of a father—he'd suddenly leaped on the biggest boy, ready to take them all on at once. They'd creamed him, of course, leaving him with a bloody nose and two black eyes. When they'd dropped him on the sidewalk at the end, he'd cracked his head open, resulting in that scar, a constant reminder of his humiliation.

That was probably the last time I stood up for myself, he realized. *At least until now . . .*

"I suppose you're right, Paula," Dexter's mother said uncertainly. "But if he's not going to be a doctor, then what is he going to do with this expensive education?"

Dexter opened his mouth to respond. Maybe now they were ready to listen to his ideas about becoming an English professor or maybe a writer. After all, he certainly seemed to be showing a talent for spinning stories lately.

"What about law school?" Aunt Paula put in before he could speak. "I heard somewhere that lots of people who are good in English and other useless subjects wind up as lawyers."

"Oh, that sounds wonderful!" Dexter's mother's expression brightened with relief. "Lawyers make almost as much money as doctors, right?"

"Sure," Aunt Paula said, sounding as confident as if she actually knew what she was talking about. "Some of 'em make even more."

"But, Mom," Dexter protested. "I don't think I—"

"Just thought of another good one," Aunt Paula interrupted, hardly seeming to remember that Dexter was in the room as she talked to her sister. "What about those real rich fellows in New York City—you know, on Wall Street? Dexy could do that. Like Donald Trump, you know?"

At that moment the program on TV broke for commercials, and an ad for a local political race came on. Dexter's mother pointed to it. "Or what about politics?" she suggested.

"I dunno if there's much money in that," Aunt Paula mused. "But we could look into it, I suppp—"

"Hey!" Dexter cried, cutting her off. The two of them turned to stare at him in surprise, and he felt his face go beet-red. "Don't I get any say in this?"

"Well, of course, Dexy," his mother said soothingly. "What do you think? How does it sound, being a lawyer?"

"Terrible." Dexter glared at her. "I'm not interested in that at all. Why should I decide to major in something I have no interest in doing?"

"Look, do you think I was interested in going in to work at that drugstore every damn day for twenty-three years?" Aunt Paula scowled at him. "Grow up, boy. Sometimes people gotta do things they ain't crazy about if they want to get by."

"I know that," Dexter said. "But—"

"But nothing." His aunt's voice was unyielding and cold. "Long as I'm footing the bills, you ain't gonna throw away your expensive education on something stupid. That sort of thing is for rich boys who can live off their trust funds. In case you haven't noticed, that category don't include you."

His mother waggled her hands soothingly at the two of them. "Now, now, you two," she murmured. "If we just talk this out . . ."

Dexter stood silently for a moment, still glaring at his aunt. Why had he ever thought she could be reasonable about this or consider his wishes? That wasn't the way she was made, and he knew it. Part of him wanted to rebel, to throw her stupid money back in her face and insist on living his own life his own way.

Almost immediately, he shrank back from that idea. Rejecting her money—and her manipulation—would feel good in the short term. But where would it leave him in the end?

Right back here where I started, he realized with a sinking feeling in his gut. *Stuck in this depressed, dead-end town with no prospects, no future . . . and no Daisy.*

He gulped, realizing how close he'd been to risking everything he'd come to care about over the past few months. So what if his aunt was close-minded and unreasonable? That wasn't exactly breaking news. He'd spent his whole life working around her stubbornness. He should be able to strike a compromise they could all live with on this matter, too. After all, wasn't he supposed to be the smart one in the family?

"All right," he said, keeping his voice as calm and reasonable as possible. "I understand. But is there maybe something else that could pay the bills besides being a doctor or lawyer or stockbroker? There are tons of different kinds of jobs out there that pay decently."

"That's the right spirit, Dexy." Once again, his mother sounded relieved. "What do you say, Paula?"

Aunt Paula seemed suspicious, but she agreed to discuss it. The three of them spent the next hour poring over the university's course catalog and hashing out Dexter's skills and interests. More than once he was tempted to get up and walk out, especially when Aunt Paula insulted him or belittled his ideas. But every time the urge struck he thought of Daisy's pretty, laughing face and bit his tongue. He could be strong for her. For them.

"It's decided, then," Aunt Paula said at last, leaning back so suddenly that the sofa squeaked in protest. "You'll major in Psychology."

Dexter didn't like the way she made it sound like a royal decree. But he was satisfied enough with the content of her remark to ignore the delivery. "Okay," he agreed. "Psych it is."

His mother clapped her hands. "Good!" she cried. "That way you can still be a doctor, Dexy. Sort of, anyway."

Dexter nodded and smiled blandly. He still didn't feel much interest in going into clinical practice, but he figured he could work that out later. As far as he was concerned, the good news was that Psych required fewer core classes than Pre-med, which meant more electives free for English Lit or Philosophy or anything else he felt like exploring—and Aunt Paula couldn't possibly complain about it.

It's not the perfect solution, he told himself, trying not to feel like a sellout for letting the women talk him down from his original plans. *But it'll do for now. And who knows—Psych just might turn out to be my thing. More likely than chemistry, anyway.* . . .

"That's true," Aunt Paula said in response to the other woman's comment. "Those shrinks make plenty, too, from what I hear." She glanced toward the muted TV, where a dapper attorney was arguing a case in front of a courtroom. "Plus if he decides to give law school a try, he can probably do that with a Psychology major just as easy as anything else, right?"

"Sure," Dexter said, though she wasn't really talking to him. When it came right down to it, he was willing to agree to just about anything as long as he was allowed to drop the hard sciences that had been the only really miserable part of his otherwise amazing first semester. Whatever else Aunt Paula demanded, he could live with it—for now, at least.

Even if it made him feel a little less like SuperDexter and a little more like a coward.

15

THE GAPING MAW OF the fuselage lay before him, the pale crimson light of the sinking sun making it glow like the gates of Hell. Dexter did his best to banish such fanciful impressions as he switched on his flashlight and took a tentative step forward. The breeze shifted and blew out at him through the husk of the plane, nearly choking him with the thick smells of jet fuel, moldy food, and rotting flesh. He gagged, not sure he could go any closer to that stench without losing the meager contents of his stomach.

It took a moment to get his churning guts back under control. Gripping his flashlight more tightly, he moved forward again, playing the beam over the closest section of the plane. He definitely wanted to see exactly where he was going in there.

No surprises, he thought with a shudder, remembering the way he'd literally stumbled over Jason's body.

The fuselage lay at a crazy upside-down angle, one at which

no airplane was meant to land. The baggage compartment was now at the top, with the passenger compartment below, its seats hanging almost straight down from the floor overhead. The ground—formerly the ceiling of the plane—was cluttered with clothing and seat cushions and bits of metal and various other parts of the plane.

Dexter took one cautious step inside, then another, holding his small flashlight before him like a weapon. Flies were everywhere, their constant buzzing drone surrounding him and blocking out any noise from outside. The oxygen masks still hung limply from their clear tubes, and Dexter shuddered as he remembered grabbing frantically for his while the plane screamed toward the ground. As he took another step he noticed a man's foot sticking out from beneath a battered metal snack cart wedged in among the wreckage, and quickly averted his eyes.

Just take a look around, then get out, Dexter told himself, breathing as shallowly as he could in a futile attempt to avoid the stench.

It got darker and harder to see his way through the rubble as he moved farther into the body of the plane, step by careful step. As he swept his light around, he noticed that most of the overhead bins—which weren't overhead anymore—were yawning open, revealing suitcases and clothes and other items within. Dexter momentarily wondered if his carry-on bag was still in its compartment, but he quickly banished the thought. It wasn't worth staying in this hellhole any longer than necessary—not for a few pairs of clean underwear and some deodorant.

As he climbed over a beam lying in his way, the buzzing chorus of flies momentarily gave way to another sound— *scritch, scritch, scratch.*

Dexter paused, his heart thumping as he listened intently for a repeat of the noise. Was he hearing things, or was there something up ahead in the dark? He told himself it was probably just more insects or perhaps rats. The thought of rats skittering in here among the dead bodies was repulsive, yet also much more comforting than some of the alternatives that popped into his head.

Don't spook yourself, Dexter told himself firmly. *There's nothing alive in here except me, about a million flies, and maybe a few rats or mice or other creepy-crawlies.*

He stepped forward again. The floor angled upward slightly, and as he climbed over more wreckage he had to hold onto the hanging seat backs for leverage. The fabric of the cushions felt damp and slightly gritty, and he let go as soon as possible.

Scritch, scratch.

The sound came again, a little louder this time. Or was it only closer?

Dexter froze in place once again. His heart was pounding so loudly that it made it even more difficult to hear the faint scratching sound.

He shone his flashlight here and there, though its tiny beam barely penetrated the darkness just a few feet ahead. Its weak white light showed crumpled sheet metal, a broken restroom sign, miscellaneous garbage. Everything he expected to find.

So why was he holding his breath, as if waiting for a mysterious figure to step out of the darkness? A figure with angry eyes in his own face . . .

He shuddered, trying to banish the image. This wasn't the time or place to worry about his mysterious doppelganger. He was here to look for Daisy, nothing more.

That reminded him . . . He flicked his light around again, forcing himself to look directly at several bodies lying here and there beneath the rubble. Several times the resulting sights brought bile into his throat, but he choked it down each time and moved on. Trying not to think about what his girlfriend might look like if he were to find her here, he kept looking, row by row.

Scritch, scritch, scratch.

Dexter gritted his teeth, determined to ignore the sound this time. Then, suddenly, something bumped against his head and he jumped, his heart nearly leaping out of his chest as he imagined a greedy hand clutching at him, dragging him off somewhere into the darkness. . . . In his panic, he tripped over his own feet and fell heavily onto a pile of rubble, sending a cloud of choking dust upward. Shining the flashlight upward through the dusty air, he saw what had grabbed at him—it was only the dangling metal end of a seatbelt.

Thump.

The last noise, louder than the rest, made him jump again and almost drop his flashlight. That hadn't sounded much like a rat. . . .

"H-hello?" he called out softly, feeling slightly foolish even in the midst of his fear. He climbed slowly to his feet, waving away the dust with his free hand. "Anybody in here?"

"Nobody but us chickens," a low voice spoke from somewhere ahead in the darkness.

Dexter bit back a scream and the impulse to run for his life. "Who is that?" he demanded sharply, ashamed to note that his voice shook as he said it. "Who's up there?"

He aimed his flashlight toward the source of the voice. Suddenly a much stronger beam shone out, blinding him for a moment. He squinted, stepping aside to try to escape from the merciless glare and nearly tripping again.

A man scooted out from his position over one of the open

overhead bins. He was tall, lean, and blond, with a sardonic smile, and Dexter recognized him right away. His name was Sawyer, and Dexter had overheard him offering to sell cigarettes to one of the other castaways earlier that day.

"Oh, it's you," Dexter said, almost collapsing with relief. "What are you doing in here?"

"I might ask you the same question," Sawyer drawled. "Jack send you in to spy on me or something?"

"Jack?" Dexter repeated. "What do you mean?"

Sawyer shrugged lazily, dragging a bulging knapsack out into view beside him. "You can tell the doc I came back for more if you want," he said. "Doesn't make no difference to me. I've got as much right to this stuff as he does, and he knows it as well as I do."

Dexter had no idea what Sawyer was talking about. "Okay, whatever," he muttered, backing away. "I'll just leave you to it, then."

Sawyer was staring at him curiously. "So you know what *I'm* doing here," he said. "But you still didn't tell me what *you're* doing here. Lookin' for something?"

Dexter didn't bother to tell him that the first part of his comment wasn't exactly true. He also didn't feel much like enlightening him on the second part. Something about the way Sawyer was watching him made him very uneasy.

"Nothing," he said. "Just, uh, looking for someone, that's all."

Not waiting for a response, he turned and went slip-sliding hurriedly back down the tilted metal floor/roof. He dodged the fallen snack cart and jumped over a pile of unrecognizable debris, finally bursting out of the dark, smelly, buzzing interior into the relatively cool and fresh twilight air outside.

He didn't look back as he hurried away from the plane. Still, he couldn't quite seem to shake the image of Sawyer, his eyes glittering in the flashlight's beam as he watched Dexter warily, sizing him up. The selfish, naked cunning in the man's eyes reminded Dexter of someone—though he couldn't for the life of him recall who that might be.

16

DEXTER STARED STRAIGHT INTO his aunt's cunning gray eyes, trying to avoid giving away his latest lie. ". . . and so I have to head back to campus a day early to make up that part of the exam."

He was a little surprised by how casual and ordinary the excuse sounded. Not sure whether to be impressed or disturbed by his increasing proficiency at lying, he waited to see if she bought it.

Aunt Paula shrugged, turning away to glance at the TV, which was blaring out her latest soap opera. "You gotta do what you gotta do," she said. "Guess you'll just have to make it up to us at spring break, eh, Dexy?"

"Sure," Dexter said, relieved that she didn't seem suspicious. His mother had accepted his excuse without question as well.

Guess I'm getting pretty good at lying, he thought as he hurried out of the room. *Must be all the practice I've had lately.*

He felt a familiar twinge of guilt. As much as he tried to pass it off in his mind as "creating his own new reality," it really was just lying. It didn't bother him much at all to deceive Aunt Paula, and deceiving his mother only troubled him a little—he suspected that not only would she forgive him if she knew, but she might even understand.

But the more time passed, the worse he felt about the other person entangled in his lies. Daisy.

What choice do I have? he thought, picturing her laughing face. *If I hadn't done it, there's no way we'd be together now.*

As soon as he was back on campus, he felt a little better about the whole situation. This was why he was doing it, after all. Someday perhaps he would figure out a way to blend his two worlds without ruining everything. In the meantime, he just had to keep all the balls in the air and hope that his luck would hold.

And his luck was about to undergo its next big test— Daisy's family. Dexter took a deep breath and straightened his shirt collar as he paused in the lobby of an expensive Italian restaurant located just off campus. He was supposed to meet Daisy and her parents there. While he couldn't wait to see Daisy again—the three weeks without her had felt like three years—he was nervous about facing her family. What would they think of him? Would they see through him immediately, know that he wasn't good enough for their daughter?

"Can I help you?" A tired-looking middle-aged waiter wandered over, interrupting his anxious thoughts.

"Yes," Dexter said uncertainly. "Um, I'm supposed to meet someone here. . . ."

"Name?" the waiter asked, sounding bored.

"Dexter Stubbs."

The waiter raised an eyebrow. "That's the name of your party?"

"Oh! No, sorry, I thought you meant my name." Dexter smiled apologetically. "I'm meeting the Wards."

"Oh! Right this way, sir." Immediately the waiter's attitude shifted. He straightened up and shot Dexter an ingratiating smile.

Dexter followed the waiter into the dining room. He spotted Daisy right away. She was sitting with a broad-shouldered man with steel-gray hair and an elegant-looking blond woman who looked exactly the way Daisy herself probably would in about thirty years.

"Hello," Dexter said weakly as he approached.

"Dexter!" Daisy leaped out of her seat and rushed around to give him a hug. "I missed you," she whispered into his ear, her warm breath tickling his neck. Then she grabbed his hand and dragged him the last few steps to the table. "Daddy, Mother, this is Dexter Stubbs."

"Ah, Dexter." Mrs. Ward smiled graciously. "It's so nice to finally meet you. Daisy talks of you so much I feel I know you already."

"Thanks. Nice to meet you, too," Dexter said.

Meanwhile Mr. Ward had climbed to his feet. He was very tall and, when he spoke, his deep voice boomed out across the restaurant. "Mr. Stubbs," he said, extending his hand. "Pleasure, young man. Have a seat and let's get to know each other, shall we?"

After a few minutes of small talk, Dexter felt himself relaxing slightly. The Wards were a bit intimidating, as he had expected, but they were also gracious and friendly. Best of all, they seemed ready to accept him at face value, giving no signs of suspicion or disapproval.

"So Daisy tells me you're thinking about med school, Dexter," Mrs. Ward said as the waiter arrived with their entrees. "That sounds very exciting."

"Uh, actually that plan has changed a little," Dexter said, feeling awkward. "I—I'm planning to declare Psychology as my major."

Daisy glanced over at him in surprise. "Really?" she said. "That's cool. When did you decide that?"

"Over the break." Dexter shrugged. "I didn't have a chance to tell you yet—it sort of just happened."

"Psychology, eh?" Mr. Ward looked up from salting his pasta. "That's not a bad field to be in these days. Can be very lucrative in its own way."

Dexter smiled weakly. "That's what I hear."

"I keep telling Daisy she ought to major in something more practical than English Lit," Mr. Ward went on, setting down the salt and expertly spinning a few strands of linguini on the end of his fork. "Finance, Econ, even Marketing—something she can use."

"People do use English, you know, Daddy," Daisy protested, looking slightly embarrassed. She glanced at Dexter. "Sorry, Dex. Daddy gets a little obsessive about this stuff sometimes."

"Somebody has to remind you about the hard facts of life, sweetheart," Mr. Ward told her. "Money doesn't grow on trees, you know. It's important to think ahead, even if you don't think you'll ever need to worry."

Dexter felt uncomfortable. Mr. Ward's comments sounded almost like something Aunt Paula might have said.

No, not really, he told himself. *At least Mr. Ward knows what he's talking about—he earns his money. He doesn't bilk people out of it like Aunt Paula does. It's totally different.*

"So, Dexter." Mrs. Ward turned and smiled at him, obviously anxious to change the subject. She reached over and patted him on the back of the hand, her heavy diamond-studded wedding band lightly rapping his knuckles. "You haven't talked much about your family. Who are your people?"

"Um . . ." Dexter swallowed hard, his nervousness returning in a flash. But he did his best to answer coherently, spinning out the usual stories about his fictional parents' law practice and educational background.

"Oh, and guess what, Daddy?" Daisy put in. "I just recently found out that Dexter's cousin is an investment banker. Isn't that cool?"

"Interesting." Mr. Ward glanced at Dexter with a raised eyebrow. "What's his name? Maybe I know him."

Dexter gulped. "Um, it's a her, actually," he said, wishing he'd never invented that particular detail. "And she lives over in Switzerland. So you probably wouldn't know each other. . . . Her name's Pauline Smith."

"Pauline Smith in Switzerland." Mr. Ward thought for a moment, then shook his head. "Nope," he said. "Doesn't ring a bell. You should tell her to drop me an email sometime if she wants to move up to the big leagues. I could probably get her in at our Paris office, or maybe London if she prefers."

"I'll be sure to mention it to her, sir," Dexter said, relieved that he hadn't let himself get tripped up by something so minor. He was going to have to be a little more careful about his stories from now on, or he was likely to lose control of what he'd already put out there.

The rest of the meal went smoothly. As he watched the waiter bring the check, Dexter could hardly believe he'd pulled it off. It was as if he'd just taken a particularly daunting midterm on his new life and passed with flying colors.

Outside the restaurant, they all huddled together in the chilly January wind to say good-bye. The Wards had already dropped off Daisy's things at her dorm, and their Mercedes was waiting at the curb to take them back to Virginia.

"It was lovely to meet you, Dexter," Mrs. Ward said warmly, grasping his hand between her soft leather gloves. "I do hope we'll see you again soon."

"Yes, yes," Mr. Ward agreed. He'd had several glasses of wine with dinner, and his cheeks and nose had taken on a ruddy glow. "In fact, I have a terrific idea. Why don't you join us for the next school break? We've been talking about taking a family trip somewhere—probably either Tokyo or Sydney, depending how my business plans shape up."

Daisy gasped. "That's a great idea, Daddy!" She turned to Dexter with bright, eager eyes. "What do you say?"

"Um, that's so nice of you," Dexter stammered, taken unprepared. "I—I'll have to check with my family and let you know."

Mr. Ward nodded, glancing at his watch. "Come, Alicia," he told his wife. "I want to get back on the road before it's too late for me to call in to the office. . . ."

The next few minutes passed in a flurry of hugs and good-byes. Dexter stood back out of the way for most of it, watching and worrying over Mr. Ward's invitation. How was he going to handle this one?

Finally the senior Wards were gone, leaving Dexter and Daisy on their own. Daisy tucked her arm through his, huddling against him with her teeth chattering.

"Come on, let's hurry up and get back to campus," she said. "I'm freezing."

They started walking. "So your parents are nice," Dexter offered.

"Oh, they loved you, too! I could tell." Daisy tilted her head up and smiled at him. "Daddy definitely did, or he wouldn't have invited you on the trip." She shivered, though whether it was from the cold or from excitement he couldn't tell. "Won't that be incredibly fun? I hope we end up in Australia—I've never been, and I'm dying to go! Oh! And you'll probably get to meet my big brother, Jason, then, too. He works for Daddy, so he'll definitely be able to get enough time off to come along." She giggled. "You'll love him—he's totally wacko."

Dexter cleared his throat. "Yeah, sounds great," he said. "Like I said, though, I still need to check in with my family first. They probably have something planned for me then, too."

Daisy's eyes widened as she glanced up at him again. "Oh, but you have to work it out this time!" she insisted. "Don't forget, though, we might have to take a few extra days off from classes. Daddy likes for us to spend at least two full weeks wherever we go." She squeezed his arm more tightly in her own. "So will you talk to your family about it?" she wheedled. "Soon?"

"Don't worry," Dexter promised, not sure what else he could say. "I'll definitely figure something out."

That seemed to satisfy her—for the moment, at least—and Dexter quickly changed the subject to the upcoming school semester. But half his mind kept returning to the other topic, worrying it like a dog with a bone. Coming back to campus a day early had been tricky enough. How was he supposed to pull this one off?

And my family isn't the only problem this time, he reminded himself as he and Daisy strolled back toward campus. *What about hers? Sure, so I managed to stay in character and convince them that SuperDexter is the real me for an hour over dinner. But spending a couple of weeks in close quarters is another story. . . .*

"Oh, and I almost forgot—don't worry about expenses for the trip," Daisy said, abruptly interrupting her own description of her new class schedule. "Daddy will probably pay for just about everything. So you can tell your parents they'll actually be saving money by letting you go." She giggled, seeming pleased with her own observation.

Dexter gulped, realizing he hadn't even thought about that aspect of his new problem. He would never be able pay even part of his own way on a trip like that. For that matter, he didn't even have a passport.

Okay, he thought grimly. *So how is SuperDexter going to deal with this?*

For the next couple of weeks the new semester kept both of them busy enough that Dexter was able to avoid the subject of the Ward family trip most of the time. Daisy pestered him about it now and then, and he always managed to put her off, but he still couldn't seem to come up with a good solution.

One day he slid into his seat in Intro to American Literature, which they were both taking that semester, to find that Daisy had beat him there for once. She leaned over to give him a kiss as he dropped his backpack at his feet.

"Thought you weren't going to make it," she commented. "Did you ever finish the reading last night?"

Dexter reached into his backpack and pulled out his battered paperback copy of Mark Twain's *The Prince and the*

Pauper, the latest book on the class syllabus. "Just barely," he said. He grinned at her. "You know, if you weren't so distracting, I might be able to get more work done."

She giggled. "Don't give me that," she said. "You know you like being distracted!"

"Well, maybe," he teased. He set the book on his desk and reached down to pull out a notebook and a pen. When he straightened up again, he saw that she was watching him intently, her playful expression gone.

"What?" he asked, suddenly self-conscious. "Do I have dirt on my face or something?"

"No," she said somberly. "I was just thinking about how much fun we always have together. And how much fun we could have on that trip with my family."

"Oh." He gulped, feeling ambushed by the sudden change of topic. His eyes darted toward the back of the classroom, but there was no sign of the professor coming in to save him from having to answer. "Um, I told you," he said lamely. "I still have to talk to my folks about that."

Her blue eyes glistened slightly, and he saw with surprise that she was holding back tears. "Are you sure you want to go?" she asked softly. "I mean, if you don't want to spend that much time with me or whatever, please just tell me. I'd rather know the truth."

"No!" Dexter blurted out, horrified. How could she even begin to think that he didn't want to be with her any chance he got? "Don't be ridiculous. It's not like that at all!"

"It just seems like you aren't that interested in the trip." She shrugged, staring down at her desk. "We already spent one school break apart. I don't want it to become a habit, you know?"

Dexter's heart was thudding nervously, and all of a sudden his hands didn't seem to know what to do with themselves. He grabbed *The Prince and the Pauper* and squeezed it, bending the cover this way and that.

"I don't either," he said, suddenly feeling choked up. Daisy told him all the time that she loved him. But until this moment, he realized, he hadn't quite dared to believe it. Now that he realized it just might be true, he felt awed and nervous and a little confused. "And don't worry—I'll make sure it doesn't happen. I'm sure my parents will understand. . . ."

She gasped, her expression brightening. "You mean you'll come on the trip?" she asked. "For sure?"

"For sure," he assured her, smiling at the unrestrained joy in her blue eyes.

His smile faded quickly once the professor entered and called the class to order. Now that he had committed himself to the trip, he felt a sick sense of dread.

I had to do it, he told himself. *I couldn't take the chance of losing Daisy. That's the most important thing in the world. I can work out the rest somehow. . . .*

Noticing that the rest of the class were paging through their books, he picked up his own copy and opened to a random page. Even though he wasn't really taking in the words on the page, he suddenly felt a great surge of understanding for one of the protagonists he'd read about the night before, the peasant boy trapped in a world of wealth and privilege that he didn't understand.

Suddenly Dexter recalled that just about everyone in the book had been happier when the truth came out at the end. He wondered briefly if that might prove to be the case in this instance as well.

Maybe it wouldn't be the worst thing in the world if Daisy found out the real story about my life, he thought, glancing over at her out of the corner of his eye. *After all, she already loves me . . .*

No, she doesn't. Another voice in his head, much harsher and less hopeful, interrupted the thought. *She doesn't love you. She loves SuperDexter. And you'd better not forget that if you want to keep her.*

17

DEXTER PUT AS MUCH distance between himself and the fuselage as possible, trying desperately to forget everything he'd seen there—especially Sawyer. But Sawyer's mocking gray eyes seemed to follow him no matter how quickly he walked, burning themselves into his brain like a flaming brand.

What's wrong with me? he thought, breaking into a jog as he headed down the shoreline, leaving the camp behind. *Nothing really happened back there. So why am I so freaked out?*

But he found it was impossible to reason with his own panic. Speeding up, he stumbled around a pile of boulders and almost ran into the Korean couple on the far side. The two of them glanced up at him, startled. Their argument appeared to be over, and they were now in the midst of preparing more of their island sushi. The man was arranging pieces of it on a tray, while the woman carefully scraped the slimy bits off another piece nearby.

"S-sorry," Dexter mumbled, his stomach roiling and pitching at the sight of the half-prepared slices of seafood. The rapidly fading light of the setting sun made them appear to swell and glow with a violent pink sheen. "Sorry. So sorry."

The man said something in Korean, sounding concerned. But even if he'd been speaking English, Dexter wasn't sure he would have been able to stand there and formulate a response. Those eyes were still after him, staring out at him from back there in the ruined fuselage, and he had to get away. If he didn't, something terrible would happen. He had no idea what; he only knew he had to escape.

"I've got to go," he said, pushing past as the Korean man reached out an arm toward him, still looking worried. "Sorry."

He left the couple behind, glancing back only when he was a safe distance way. They had already turned back to their tasks, their heads bowed and close together as they worked. Dexter felt a moment of envy; the couple seemed to have carved out their own private, insular little world even in the midst of the chaos on the island. It was sort of nice—as if they were already at home here, just because they had each other.

Of course, it could also just be that nobody can understand a thing they say, he reminded himself. *For all we know, the two of them might not even be a couple. They could be total strangers, or brother and sister, or they could hate each other's guts, or they could be international spies plotting to kill us all. . . .*

He turned around again and was almost overcome with a quick attack of dizziness. His stomach reeled, his throat clenched, and somewhere in the recesses of his mind he was vaguely aware that he needed to get away from the still-stifling heat of the beach. Veering up toward the jungle, he staggered into the shelter of the trees. Before long he found himself pushing his way through a partially shaded clearing waving with pale green, chest-high grass. The blades were surprisingly stiff and sharp, still glistening with moisture from the rain earlier that day.

Beyond the grassy area lay a grove of mature trees with pale, twisting trunks. It was much darker there beneath the shade of their gently swaying leaves, which blocked out most of the rays of the fading sun. As Dexter pushed blindly forward, deeper into the jungle, the image of Sawyer's sneering face slowly faded from his mind, replaced by that of a monstrously fat woman with pockmarked skin and overprocessed hair. Her eyes glared at him accusingly. *What's wrong with you, boy?* she shouted inside his head. *Don't you know who you are anymore?*

"No," he mumbled, pressing his hands against his ears as if that would shut out the woman's harangue. He had no idea who she was, but all of a sudden he was convinced that he knew her. Or had known her. Or would know her . . . It was difficult to keep track of time in his current frame of mind.

Dexter collapsed against a tree trunk to rest for a moment. Swiping away the sweat pouring down his face, he closed his eyes. But the woman's face was there, waiting. His eyes flew open again and he stared upward through the treetops, his gaze fixing on a streak of deep pink slashing across the darkening sky like a wound. For some reason the sight of it made him want to cry.

I need to get a grip, he thought, doing his best to calm his swirling mind. *Focus, Dexter. Think about something easy, something good and real. . . .*

The first image that popped into his head, of course, was

Daisy. He concentrated on her cheerful, beautiful, familiar face, lovingly drinking in every curve of her cheeks and swell of her lips. But after a moment the happy Daisy face started to frown, and within seconds her delicate features were twisted into a deep, furious scowl.

Dexter recoiled from the image, feeling shocked and anxious . . . and guilty, though he wasn't sure why. Did it have something to do with that fight back in Sydney, the argument he couldn't quite seem to remember?

"What's the matter?" he asked the image of Daisy in his head. "Please, Daisy—tell me what's wrong so I can fix it. Tell me what we fought about back in Sydney. . . ."

His voice broke, and he let out a sob of frustration. In some distant corridor of his brain, he knew that he was dehydrated again and getting delirious. But instead of making him feel sick as usual, it was also making him feel lost and out of place and confused.

Dexter . . . !

The ghost of a voice echoed around him, and he wasn't sure if it was coming from inside his head or somewhere out in the jungle. "Daisy?" he whispered uncertainly.

He staggered to his feet, staring around frantically. Was she here? Had he found her at last?

Dexter . . . !

The whisper was more urgent this time. "I'm coming, Daisy! I'm here!" he shouted.

He burst into motion, racing deeper into the jungle. More than once he tripped over a root or a rock, only to catch himself against a tree and keep going. His breath came in ragged gasps, the air feeling as thick as water in his lungs. But he didn't stop—he couldn't stop. He was convinced that Daisy was waiting for him just ahead—around that next tree, the next bend in the trail. . . .

He had to find her. That was the only thing that would make everything better. He knew it as well as he knew his own name.

Finally he rounded a tangled thicket of vines and spied a flash of blond hair in the clearing just beyond. "Daisy!" he blurted out, his heart filling with relief. "Daisy, it's me! Wait!"

He lunged into the clearing, panting with relief. Then he stopped short, his breath freezing in his throat. There in the clearing, standing right next to Daisy with one protective hand on her shoulder, was . . . him. The other Dexter.

"What are you doing out here?" the other Dexter demanded, dropping his hand from Daisy's arm and stepping forward.

"I—I came to find Daisy," Dexter blurted out. "Daisy, it's me—it's Dexter."

"*I'm* Dexter," the other one said, his words echoing ominously inside Dexter's head. He tugged on the slightly ragged hem of his shirt with his free hand. "And you'd better not ever forget it. Because I'll always be the real Dexter, no matter what you do."

"No!" Dexter cried in alarm. "Daisy, don't listen to him—he's lying."

"She knows the truth," the other Dexter said calmly. "She knows that I'm not the one who's lying. Not like you. You're pathetic. You hide yourself behind a fake identity and a fake name. Why would anyone want a fake?"

"I don't know what you're talking about," Dexter protested weakly. Still, something about the other Dexter's words filled his insides with loathing and shame. Could it be true? But how? "Daisy?" he pleaded, turning toward her with his hands outspread. "Please, Daisy . . ."

"Dexter, what's wrong with you?" Daisy stared at him, her upper lip curling with distaste. "Snap out of it! Geez!"

"Real sympathetic. But seriously, Dexter." The taunting tone of Other Dexter's voice was fading in and out like static on the radio, leaving behind only concern and anxiety. "I think we'd better get you back to the beach."

Dexter blinked as the other Dexter's face swam and melted, blurring out of recognition. "What—what's happening?" he whispered.

He put both hands over his eyes, pressing hard. Colorful squiggles and sparks danced behind his lids. Then the face of the fat woman was back, wearing Sawyer's mocking smile and chewing on a piece of the Korean couple's seafood. Weird, disjointed images tumbled through Dexter's mind like the pingpong numbers in the big glass bin on that lottery program . . . the program his aunt watched almost every day in hopes that her luck would change. . . .

My aunt . . . he thought, confused, as the fat woman's face leered at him again. *Aunt Paula* . . .

He heard a sound and opened his eyes just in time to see the other Dexter make a sudden moved toward him. Dexter took a step back, suddenly certain that the other version of him was moving in for the kill, planning to swallow him up and take him over.

"No!" he cried, lifting both hands to defend himself. "Don't hurt me! I'm you—I'm still you!"

"Dexter?" As the other guy grabbed his arm, his face suddenly shimmered and then rearranged itself into a completely different set of features.

"Boone?" Dexter said uncertainly. Glancing toward the spot where Daisy had stood just a moment ago, he saw only Shannon staring back at him with open astonishment. "Shannon? What are you guys doing here?"

"Don't try to talk, buddy." Boone put a supporting arm around his shoulders. "We'd better get you back to the beach so Jack can take a look at you."

"But, but Daisy . . ."

"Heads up, Boone—he's falling!"

Daisy . . . Dexter's mind couldn't hold onto the thought any longer. He gave up, watching it flutter off into the ether like a butterfly. Then he slumped against Boone's arm as his consciousness started to go sparkly-gray and fuzzy around the edges.

18

"HEADS UP, DEXO!"

Dexter turned just in time to avoid getting beaned in the head with the can of soda Jason had just winged at him from the other side of the pool. He caught the can, then smiled weakly as Daisy's brother guffawed loudly at his surprised expression.

"Grow up, Jase," Daisy scolded mildly from her beach towel. "You're not a frat boy anymore, remember?"

"Once a frat boy, always a frat boy." Jason's fleshy lips drew back in a grin, and he tossed Dexter a mischievous wink. Then he raced forward and did a front flip into the pool, splashing Daisy and making her shriek.

Dexter forced a chuckle. It was only a couple of days into their trip to Sydney, and he was already weary of Jason's antics. Daisy's older brother was gregarious and fun-loving, just as she had described him. The trouble was, his behavior often verged on obnoxious. He was twenty-three years old, but his sense of humor seemed to have stalled out at around age thirteen.

Mrs. Ward looked over the tops of her sunglasses, shifting her position on one of the hotel pool's chaises. "Now, Jason," she said mildly as her son popped up out of the water and floated toward the edge of the pool. "Don't cause trouble, do you hear me?" Setting down the magazine she was reading, she sat up and stretched, then glanced around. "This is a lovely pool, isn't it?"

"Yeah," Dexter agreed truthfully. The pool—and the whole hotel—were nicer than anything he ever could have imagined. The three-room suite the Wards had booked was larger than his mother's entire house.

He winced, thinking about his mother. She had sounded genuinely sad when he'd called to tell her he would be spending this school break on a study-abroad internship. But once Aunt Paula had heard that it could lead to a lucrative job after graduation, she'd quickly convinced her sister that it was the best thing for Dexter to do.

I wish I hadn't had to lie to them, though, Dexter thought uneasily. *It seems like just about everything I say these days is a lie. . . .*

Despite his misgivings, he had to admit that the trip to Sydney was going quite smoothly so far. To his relief, the Wards had insisted on covering all of Dexter's expenses, including the pricey plane ride—in business class, no less. Since arriving in Australia, Mr. Ward had spent most of his time working, leaving the rest of them to sightsee, shop, and sit by the pool. At the end of the week, the senior Wards were continuing on to Japan, where Mr. Ward had further business. But Daisy and Jason— and, therefore, Dexter—had opted to remain in Sydney and fly home separately. Dexter was looking forward to spending those few days with Daisy, out from under the watchful eye of her parents. Of course, he would still have to deal with Jason . . .

Dexter popped open the soda Jason had tossed. It fizzed and bubbled over, and he quickly grabbed his towel to catch the mess. His copy of *The Prince and the Pauper,* which had been lying on the towel, went flying onto the ground.

Mrs. Ward leaned over and retrieved the book. She glanced at the cover. "Mark Twain, hmm?" she said. "Are you enjoying it, Dexter?"

"Sure," he replied. "Actually we read it earlier this semester. But I decided to feature it in my midterm paper, which is due pretty soon after we get back. So I brought it along to review."

She paged through it, nodding. "I read this one in college, too," she said. "It's an interesting story. What's your paper going to be about?"

"Leave him alone, Ma," Jason spoke up before Dexter could answer. He was in the water at the edge of the pool, his thick, tanned arms resting on the cement edging. "Dexo's here to have fun, not to talk to the old folks about school."

Mrs. Ward looked slightly hurt. "No one's forcing you to listen, Jason," she murmured mildly. "Sorry if I'm boring you."

"Yeah, stuff it, Jase," Daisy muttered.

There was an awkward moment of silence. Dexter felt oddly guilty, even though he hadn't done anything wrong. He wondered if he should ignore what Jason had said and answer Mrs. Ward's question. Then again, he wasn't sure he wanted to discuss Twain's tale about the lives of the very rich and very poor with her. Now that he thought about it, it seemed a little too close to his own life lately.

Finally Mrs. Ward sighed and stood up. "I suppose I'll go

shower," she said. "Your father said he should be through with his meeting in time to have dinner with the family tonight."

"We'll be in soon, Mother," Daisy said. As soon as Mrs. Ward was gone, Daisy rounded on her brother. "You don't have to be such a jerk to her," she snapped. "She and Daddy *are* paying for you to be on this trip, you know."

Jason shrugged, looking sullen. "Chill, spaz girl. I was just kidding around. She knows that."

Daisy sighed and stood up, gathering her things. "Come on, Dexter," she said. "I'm getting sick of swimming."

Two hours later, all five of them were dressed for dinner and in a much better mood. Whatever tension and hard feelings had afflicted the Wards earlier apparently had been forgotten by everyone except Dexter. Daisy, Jason, and their parents chatted and joked around easily as they entered a candlelit seafood restaurant just a couple of blocks from their hotel. They were seated immediately at a private table in a pleasant garden courtyard out back.

"So," Mr. Ward said abruptly, turning to address Dexter. "How's the psychology business these days, young man?"

Even though Mr. Ward had been nothing but nice, he still made Dexter feel uncomfortable. It was as if the two of them were always speaking slightly different languages—or at least different dialects. He couldn't quite put his finger on why he felt that way, but he couldn't seem to shake it, and it always left him feeling a bit off-kilter when Mr. Ward spoke to him.

"Just fine, sir," Dexter said politely. "I'm really enjoying the psych class I'm taking this semester. My professor is pretty cool, too. He was just telling me I should think about grad school, maybe going into research or something."

"That's fine," Mr. Ward said, tucking his napkin in his lap.

"But if you do it, make sure you get into the corporate side. You don't want to get stuck in the academic ghetto. You're a smart kid—you deserve to live a comfortable life."

"Oh, Daddy." Daisy, who had been listening, rolled her eyes. "Don't listen to him, Dexter. He thinks everything outside of Wall Street is some kind of ghetto."

Dexter smiled uncomfortably as the others chuckled knowingly. He was starting to think that his impression during that first dinner had been right—Mr. Ward's constant references to money still reminded him of Aunt Paula, even though the two of them were worlds apart in every other way.

Mr. Ward waved away a fly that was buzzing around him, then glanced across the table at his son. "Too bad Jason didn't seem to inherit my interest in business," he commented. "If he'd had his way, he'd be playing the guitar in some dive bar right now and living at the YMCA."

Jason snorted. "Give it a rest, Dad," he said irritably. "You won, okay? I'm working for your company. So quit with the guilt trip already."

"Enough arguing, everyone." Mrs. Ward's voice was as soft as ever, but her tone was forceful nonetheless. "We're supposed to be having a nice, relaxing vacation. Now let's talk about something pleasant, shall we?"

The others didn't resist as she started chatting about their sightseeing plans for the next day. For the rest of the meal they discussed that and other innocuous topics. Later, as the senior Wards went back to the hotel bar for a drink and Jason wandered off in search of a video arcade, Dexter and Daisy took a private stroll through the evening streets of Sydney. It was a warm evening with just a hint of a breeze, and Dexter almost immediately felt himself relaxing.

"This is nice," Daisy murmured after a moment.

"Yeah." Dexter glanced around, enjoying the feel of the slight breeze off the harbor. "Sydney's a pretty cool place. But it's weird . . ." He trailed off thoughtfully.

"What?" she said. "You mean the architecture and stuff?"

He shrugged. "Yeah, sort of," he said. "But that's just it. Every time we walk around a corner and see that famous opera house, or go into a store that's playing didgeridoo music, or overhear people talking in that Aussie accent, it feels really foreign and exotic. But then other times, like this . . ." He waved a hand at the quiet streets around them—"We could be in any city, anywhere in the world. At least that's how it feels, you know?"

She smiled. "Sure," she said. "I know what you mean."

Dexter was still thinking. "Maybe cities are sort of like people that way. They may look different on the outside, but they have a lot in common underneath."

"Ooh, deep," she teased. "Did you learn that in Psych class?"

Dexter blushed and grinned. "Maybe," he teased back.

They walked on in friendly silence for a moment. Suddenly Dexter found himself wishing that the moment could stretch on and on, maybe forever. He and Daisy could just stay there, together and happy and smiling and understanding each other. But almost before the thought came, he realized with a pang of regret that it couldn't be. Soon, all too soon, they would be returning to the cares of school and daily life and family . . .

"By the way, I—I like your family," he said, breaking the silence. "At first I was pretty intimidated by them, because they seemed so perfect. But then I found out you guys argue and stuff, just like everybody else."

Daisy glanced over at him. "Of course we do," she said. "What did you think? I mean, we *are* just like everyone else."

"Yeah . . ." Suddenly, walking along with her through the quiet, moonlit streets of that strange-yet-familiar city, Dexter was overcome with the almost irresistible urge just to blurt out the truth.

I need to tell her sometime, he thought. *This SuperDexter stuff is working for now. But it can't go on forever.*

"Anyway, I can't wait to meet *your* family," she said, pressing up against him and smiling up at him. "I want to figure out exactly where you got that handsome face and adorable personality from. Maybe we can pop into New York sometime before the end of term and have dinner with them or something."

He smiled weakly. "Yeah," he said, realizing the moment for truth had just drifted past like dry leaves in the evening breeze. "That sounds like fun."

On Mr. and Mrs. Ward's last evening before they flew to Japan, Mr. Ward pulled Dexter aside after dinner at the hotel restaurant. "I'd like to talk to you for a moment, son," he said in his usual commanding manner. "My wife and I will be leaving Sydney soon, and you and I haven't really had a chance to talk. You know—man to man."

Dexter flinched. He didn't like the sound of that. "Of course," he replied.

The two of them paused while Daisy, Jason, and Mrs. Ward walked on ahead across the lobby. Dexter pasted a polite half-smile on his face and waited, bracing himself for more difficult questions about himself and his background.

Instead Mr. Ward started rambling on about his own life. He talked about growing up all over the world as the son of a diplomat, about his college days, and then his successful career in high finance.

"You see where I'm going with this, don't you, my boy?" he said, glancing quizzically at Dexter.

"Um . . ." Dexter wasn't sure what to say.

Fortunately, Mr. Ward barely paused before continuing. "So you know the reason I did it all?" he said. "The money, the comfortable house . . . It was for my family. For Alicia, and later for Jason and Daisy. They mean the world to me, Dexter. And that's why I want to give them the world."

Dexter still had no idea how to respond. "That's—great, sir," he said uncertainly. "I'm sure they appreciate that."

The man nodded and clapped Dexter on the shoulder. "Yes. And that's why I appreciate *you,* young man," he said. "I like seeing you with Daisy. I can tell you have a good head on your shoulders, and that you're going places. You remind me a little of myself at your age. And I know you'll take care of Daisy just as I always have. I just wanted to tell you that."

"Thanks," Dexter said uneasily. He could tell that Mr. Ward was a little drunk—once again, he'd had several glasses of wine with dinner. But his words still rang true to form.

It all comes back to money with him, Dexter realized with a sinking feeling in his gut. *That's just who he is . . . and it's how Daisy was raised. Mr. Ward would never be able to accept the real me. And maybe I'm kidding myself to think that Daisy ever could, either.*

19

FOR A FEW MINUTES Dexter wasn't sure if the near-constant moans and groans he heard were coming from himself or not. It was all he could do to stay conscious and focus on swallowing the cool sips of water someone kept giving him. He was lying flat on his back on the sand a few yards from one of the signal fires. Opening his eyes with some effort, he stared up at the expanse of sky overhead. It was just melting from deep blue into a darker twilight gray, and the stars appeared to be blinking on one by one as he watched.

"Here you go, Dex." Arzt's concerned face came into view, blocking the stars as he peered down at him. He put the water bottle to Dexter's lips. "Try to take another few swallows. Jack says it's the only thing that will help."

Dexter lifted his head and did as Arzt said. The water tasted good, and even those few sips cleared his head a little more. After a moment he felt good enough to sit up.

"Ugh," he said, putting a hand to his throbbing head. "Thanks, man. I guess the heat really wasted me this time." He heard another shout of pain, and this time was pretty sure it hadn't come from him. "Is that the shrapnel guy?"

Arzt grimaced. "Yeah. I'm starting to think that whatever Jack's doing for him, it ain't working."

There was another loud groan. Dexter shuddered and sucked down another mouthful of water, trying not to listen.

When he glanced around the beach, he could tell most of the people there were doing the same. Claire and Charlie were standing together near one of the other fires, their backs turned toward the infirmary tent. Boone and Shannon had been coming over occasionally to see how Dexter was doing since bringing him back to camp. They were spending the rest of their time wandering around nearby, talking to each other in low voices and occasionally shooting anxious glances toward the tent. Sayid was standing alone a little ways away, staring straight toward the source of the groans with worry in his eyes.

Then Dexter saw one person who didn't seem to be paying any attention at all to the noises. George was hurrying toward him with a smile on his broad, ruddy face. He was carrying a dark, battered-looking suitcase, which was no surprise—he had assigned himself the task of gathering all the luggage he could find on the first day, and was still keeping himself busy finding scattered bits and pieces in the jungle and farther down the beach.

"Dexter!" he called out. "There you are, buddy. I've been looking all over for you."

"You found me," Dexter said with a weary smile as the man reached him. "What's up?"

"This look familiar?" George held up the dark suitcase.

Once the firelight illuminated it, Dexter gasped. "That looks like mine!" he cried. "I can't believe you found it—I'd pretty much given up."

George shrugged. "Was hoping it might be yours," he said. "I wasn't sure—see, the tag here on the handle says 'Dexter Stubbs,' but I figured, how many Dexters could there be on this island?"

Dexter froze. The last puzzle piece had just fallen into place in his mind with a reverberating *thud*.

"Dexter Stubbs?" Arzt said, his voice seeming to echo across the beach. Or perhaps that was only in Dexter's head . . . "So is your name Dexter Cross, or Dexter Stubbs?"

"I—" Dexter's throat had gone dry again, but this time he was sure no amount of water would help. The truth was all flooding back now, so sharp and real that he could hardly believe he hadn't remembered sooner. "I—I guess that's my real name. Dexter Stubbs."

Dexter squeezed his eyes shut. Now that the truth was out, he wasn't sure he could stand it. It was no wonder he'd tried to forget it all. No wonder he'd tried to wipe the slate clean and start anew on this island.

When he opened his eyes, Boone was rubbing his chin, looking stunned. Arzt and George were staring at Dexter with naked curiosity. Out of the corner of his eye, Dexter could see Shannon wandering toward them. Charlie and Claire were looking his way, too, as if wondering what all the commotion was about.

He glanced helplessly at Arzt. Was that suspicion and distrust he saw in his eyes?

Suddenly unable to bear the shame of it all, Dexter pushed himself to his feet. His head spun woozily, but he ignored it.

"Excuse me," he muttered, his face hot with humiliation. "I—I've got to go."

Not looking at anyone, he raced away up the beach. A few people called out his name, but he didn't slow down even when he reached the jungle. He kept running, pushing his way blindly through the near-darkness, tripping on roots but hardly feeling the pain. The groans of the dying man seemed to follow him, echoing inside his head to match his mood.

I didn't know how good I had it, he thought bleakly, crashing through a thick stand of bamboo. *If only I still had the amnesia. Then maybe I could still believe in that better life I invented for myself. Maybe I could lose myself in the fantasy of SuperDexter, at least for a little while longer . . .*

20

DEXTER CLOSED HIS EYES, losing himself in the loud, pulsing music of the Sydney club. He was vaguely aware of Daisy dancing beside him, her blond hair damp with sweat and her face blissfully happy.

"Yo, dude!" Jason shouted suddenly in Dexter's ear, causing his eyes to fly open. "This place rocks, doesn't it?"

Dexter grinned and gave him a thumbs-up, not bothering to try to make himself heard over the pounding blast of the oversized speakers. It was their last night in Sydney, and at first Dexter had been annoyed at Jason's insistence that they all go clubbing. He'd been picturing a much quieter, more romantic evening featuring himself and Daisy; perhaps a nice dinner, followed by a look out over the city from the observation deck of the Sydney Tower.

But he'd soon realized that wasn't going to happen, and since Daisy had seemed excited at the chance to go dancing,

Dexter had given in without a fight. And he'd even discovered a silver lining—Jason was a lot easier to take after five or six drinks. Or maybe it was seven. He'd stopped keeping track after a while. What difference did it make? He could sleep it off on the long flight home the next day.

Daisy leaned up against him, standing on tiptoes to speak into his ear. "This is fun!" she shouted. "I can't believe we have to leave tomorrow. Back to the real world!"

Dexter nodded and planted a kiss on her sweat-dampened cheek. "At least we'll always have Sydney!" he shouted back with a grin.

She giggled, though he couldn't hear it over the music. *Be right back,* she mouthed, gesturing toward the restrooms and then pushing her way through the crowd.

He watched her until she disappeared from view, then glanced around at the throngs of fashionably dressed young people bumping and grinding all around him. With a flash of pride, he realized that nobody watching would ever be able to guess that he hadn't been born into this world, or that he couldn't even have afforded the cover charge to get into a club like this just a year earlier.

His gaze shifted to the mirrored back wall. Locking onto his own eyes, he felt his smile fade slightly. For a long, breathless moment the noise of the club faded in his mind, and all he could do was stare at his own reflection. Was it a trick of the light, some weird reflection of the mirrored disco ball that cast that moody shadow over his face or made his eyes look so dark and troubled? He drifted a little closer, but nothing changed. The eyes looking back at him were watchful and deceptive and eerily unfamiliar . . .

"I'm back!" Daisy appeared at his side, shattering his

intense focus on his own face. She jumped up and down, grinning eagerly. "Come on!" she shouted breathlessly, gesturing toward the exit. "Let's grab Jase and go find some new fun!"

A few minutes later the three of them were walking down the street outside. Dexter's head was still pounding with the echoes of the overly loud music but the relatively cool night air was a relief after the stuffy, smoky atmosphere inside the club.

"What are we going to do now?" Jason's voice sounded louder than ever as it echoed off the darkened buildings and bounced its way down the deserted street. It was very late, and there was no one else in sight.

Daisy clung to Dexter's arm, her whole body seeming to vibrate with energy. "Should we try that other club that girl told us about?" she asked. "It sounded fun."

"Do you remember where it was?" Dexter asked, stifling a yawn. The effects of those drinks were wearing off quickly, and exhaustion was settling over him like a cloak. "I don't."

"It was supposed to be just around the corner from that last place," Jason said. "Let's just walk a little farther and . . . Hey. Check out this guy."

Dexter followed Jason's gaze and saw a lean young man coming toward them. He was dressed in a ragged pair of shorts and a T-shirt that looked as if it hadn't been washed in a year. His dirty feet were shoved into a pair of faded flip-flops that were at least a couple of sizes too small, and he was holding a straw hat in one hand.

"G'day, mates," the young man said when he got a little closer. "Help a fella out?" He held out his hat hopefully.

Jason shot Dexter an evil grin. "That all depends," he said, cracking his knuckles and taking a step closer to the panhandler. "What are you willing to do for it? Hmm?"

"Look, I don't want any trouble, mate," the panhandler said, lifting both his hands in surrender. "If you don't have any coin to spare, I'll go on my way."

"Yeah, that sounds like a much better idea," Jason agreed with a smirk. "Why don't you take your reeking, worthless hide out of our way now, so we can get back to our pleasant evening?"

Dexter winced at Jason's comment. What right did he have to be so rude just because this guy didn't happen to be born rich like him?

"Knock it off, man," he told Jason sharply. Reaching into his pocket, he pulled out a crumpled bill, suddenly overcome with the weird feeling that he was acting out some vaguely recalled scene from *The Prince and the Pauper*. "Here you go, man. Sorry I don't have any—"

"Dexter!" Daisy shrieked. "Look out!"

Dexter glanced over his shoulder just in time to see an elbow flying at him. He ducked, avoiding the worst of the blow, but it still cracked into his cheek and sent him reeling. For a moment he felt woozy, and as he struggled to stay on his feet he was only vaguely aware of the sound of angry shouting from Jason and frightened screams from Daisy.

By the time his head cleared a few seconds later, it was all over. "Which way did they go?" Jason blustered, his fists at the ready. "They better run if they know what's good for them!"

Meanwhile Daisy was clutching at Dexter's shirt and stroking his face lightly. "Dexter! Are you okay?" she sobbed. "Can you hear me?"

"I—I think I'm okay." Dexter shook off the last lingering effects of the hit. "What happened?"

"That guy came up behind us and grabbed my purse," Daisy

said. "I think he was going for your wallet, too, but you saw him just in time."

"He must've been working with that beggar guy," Jason put in. "They both split as soon as I started fighting back." He scowled at the empty streets around them, but his expression faded into concern as he glanced toward his sister. "You okay, Daisy?"

"I'm okay." Her voice already sounded a little calmer. "I guess for a first mugging, that actually wasn't so bad." She gave a slightly forced-sounding laugh. "The important thing is we're all still in one piece, right?"

"Your passport wasn't in your purse, was it?" Jason asked.

Daisy shook her head. "Thank God, it's back at the hotel," she said. "But all my cash and credit cards were in there." She shook her head, looking annoyed. "What a pain. I'll have to cancel the cards right away."

Jason shrugged. "Yeah. Good thing you brought your boyfriend along to pick up the slack for the rest of the trip. Otherwise we'd all have to hitchhike to the airport tomorrow."

"What do you mean?" Dexter's whole body suddenly went cold despite the balmy air.

Jason grinned sheepishly. "I was counting on Daisy to buy me breakfast and pay for the cab and stuff," he admitted. "After buying that last round of drinks tonight, I'm totally tapped out." He clapped Dexter on the shoulder. "You don't mind fronting me a few bucks, do you, buddy? You know I'm good for it."

Dexter weakly returned Jason's grin, but he felt like throwing up. After buying himself nice new luggage for this trip, along with the passport fees and all the other little incidentals he'd had to cover himself, he barely had any money left to his name.

As the three of them started the long walk back to their hotel, he frantically ran the numbers in his head, trying to figure out whether he could cover the cab fare to the airport and other expenses. After all, they were leaving tomorrow.

No, he finally had to admit, his heart sinking. *I just don't have enough. Not for these two. They spend like money means nothing. There's no way they're going to understand if I try to keep them on a budget. Not unless I come clean . . .*

He glanced up at their hotel, which had just come into sight on the next block. As Jason surged forward eagerly, muttering something about calling the police, Dexter felt the all-too-familiar sense of defeat settle over him. He held Daisy back.

"Listen," he said slowly. It felt kind of like he was back in high school, knowing the rich bullies had cornered him and he might as well just relax and take the inevitable beating. Knowing he had no other choice. "I need to tell you something."

"Can it wait a sec?" she asked, distracted. "I should probably go with Jason so I can tell the cops what was in my purse."

"No. This can't wait."

Something in his voice must have convinced her, because she stopped and stared at him curiously. "What is it, Dexter?"

He took a deep breath. "It's about the money thing," he said softly. "See, I'm not exactly who you think I am . . ."

Once the first few words were out, the rest poured out of him in a rush—his aunt's windfall, his pathetic background, the SuperDexter plan, all of it. It almost felt good to let it go, to get it all out in the open.

Almost.

"You—you lied to me?" Daisy just stared at him when he finished, her expression shifting uncertainly between anger and heartbreak.

"I'm sorry," he said, desperate to chase away that haunted look. "But it really doesn't change anything between us. I'm still the same person, I—"

She shook her head, tears already running down her face. "No, I think I really don't know you at all," she said, her voice cracking slightly. "Or maybe it's you who doesn't know me. See, I wouldn't have minded you being poor, Dexter. I wouldn't have cared about that at all. It's the lying I can't deal with . . ."

Breaking off with a sob, she turned and raced toward the hotel. He took a few steps after her and then stopped, feeling hopeless. What good would it do to try to explain? She'd already made up her mind that he'd betrayed her trust.

And she's right, he thought miserably. *That's the worst part. She's absolutely right.*

21

ONCE HE WAS SURE nobody was following him, Dexter slowed to a walk. Glancing around the rapidly darkening jungle, he wished he'd stopped to pick up a flashlight on his way out there. Luckily the moon and stars gave just enough light to keep him from crashing into the trees.

He stopped in a small, starlit clearing and leaned against a tree. Dropping his head into his hands, he let out a small moan that blended with the groans still faintly audible from the direction of the beach.

How could I have forgotten? he wondered bleakly. *It's like I tricked myself into believing my own lies. . . .*

"Maybe that's because you wanted to believe them."

"Who said that?" Startled, Dexter dropped his hands and blinked out into the darkness. "Who's there?"

A figure stepped out of the trees on the far side of the clearing. For a second Dexter thought it might be Boone, and his heart soared. Did that mean Boone had come after him to bring him back; that Dexter wasn't going to be an outcast from camp from now on?

Then the figure took another step and Dexter saw that he was a little younger than Boone, and a little shorter. His hair was a little lighter, his eyes a little darker, his nose and chin not quite the same. . . .

Dexter's heart pounded. "Is that—is that you?" he stammered. "I mean, *me*?"

He had a lightheaded feeling, as if his mind was floating off over the treetops, untethered to reality. But the figure looked solid enough—the twigs crunched beneath his feet; the blades of grass bent as he moved across the clearing.

"You know who I am." The figure stepped into a shaft of moonlight.

Dexter stared at him. Once again he noticed that the other Dexter's clothing was a bit shabbier than his own and that his hair looked slightly different. Different, and yet somehow familiar.

"You're me," he whispered. "The *old* me."

"The *real* you," the other Dexter said, his eyes and tone accusatory. "The one you left behind the day you got that money. The one you're still ashamed of, even though I did nothing wrong."

Dexter shook his head. "But I'm not—I didn't," he protested weakly. "I—I only did what I thought would help us. Me." Once again his head spun crazily, and he wondered if he'd ever really woken from that last bout of delirium. Maybe he'd only imagined being rescued by Boone and Shannon and tended by Arzt. For that matter, who was to say that *any* of it was real? That he wasn't still sitting on that Oceanic flight as it plummeted out of the sky? For all he knew this could all be the desperate workings of his doomed mind.

Oddly, that thought made him feel a bit braver. "What do you want?" he challenged the other Dexter.

"To remind you where you came from. Who you are."

"I already remember that." This time Dexter's voice was a little stronger. "I think about it every damn day. How could I possibly forget?"

"You forgot about me."

"What?" Dexter put one hand to his forehead. It felt clammy and a little shaky. "What are you talking about?"

"I'm talking about *you,* Dexter *Cross.*" The other Dexter's tone was contemptuous. "You forgot that Dexter Stubbs ever existed."

"That was just the dehydration," Dexter protested.

"Right. And was dehydration the reason you never told Daisy the truth? She trusted you."

"I know . . ." Dexter whispered, suddenly feeling choked up as he remembered the hurt look in Daisy's eyes when he'd finally leveled with her.

"You didn't deserve her, and you know it."

Dexter didn't have an answer for that. Suddenly he felt very tired. "Look, I mean it," he said wearily. "What do you want with me?"

"I want . . ." The other Dexter paused. "I want . . ."

BANG!

Dexter jumped and spun around. Had that been a gunshot? Whatever it was, it had come from the direction of the beach. He stared intently in that direction, even though at least a hundred yards of thick foliage separated this spot from the shoreline.

"Did you hear that?" he asked. "What do you think it—"

He cut himself off as he turned around and saw that his doppelganger was gone.

"Hey," he called. "Wait!"

Had the figure been there at all? Suddenly the answer to that question seemed of paramount importance—far more important than returning to the beach to see what had happened. Rushing to the spot where the figure had stood, Dexter dropped to his hands and knees on the ground.

Footprints, he thought feverishly. *There should be footprints. . . .*

He peered at the ground, but in the faint sprinkling of starlight from overhead he couldn't see a thing. Pressing his fingers against the slightly moist ground, he felt around for indentations.

What am I doing? he thought after a moment, abruptly stopping his frantic search and sitting up on his heels. *What am I looking for here, anyway?*

Feeling foolish, he climbed to his feet. Just then he heard the crashing and snapping sound of someone moving quickly through the jungle. He squared his shoulders and took a deep breath, preparing himself for the return of his doppelganger.

Instead, Kate stepped out of the trees. She was wearing a billowy white overshirt that glowed under the pale light of the moon and stars.

"Oh!" she said, obviously startled to see him. "Dexter, is that you? Sorry, I didn't know anyone was . . ."

Her voice trailed off, and she looked away quickly. Dexter felt his face flush with shame. Had she heard about him already? Had the gossip traveled around the camp so quickly?

Then he blinked, realizing she was sniffling. "Are you okay?" he asked, momentarily forgetting his own problems.

"It's nothing," she mumbled. "The Marshall . . ."

"The what?"

"That guy in the tent." Kate's voice sounded choked up. "He . . ."

Dexter glanced in the direction of the beach, putting two and two together. "Oh. That gunshot I heard—the tent guy—is he . . ."

Kate glanced up just long enough to nod. Even in the dim light, he could see that her eyes were glistening with unshed tears.

Dexter hadn't even realized that Kate knew that guy any better than the rest of them. But whether she had or not, it was clear that whatever had happened had upset her deeply.

"Anyway," she said, sniffing sharply and swiping at her nose with the back of her hand, "I just needed to get away for a few minutes. See you."

She stepped across the clearing, heading deeper into the jungle. For a moment Dexter was ready to let her go. After all, Kate seemed like one of the smartest and most capable people on the island. What help could he expect to give her, especially when he was such a mess himself?

Still, something inside of him couldn't resist trying to help. "Do you want to talk about it?" he asked.

22

DEXTER WAS PANTING AS he entered the air-conditioned lobby. The beginnings of a sparkly aura danced at the edges of his vision, and he knew he was dehydrated—the alcohol, the warm night, and the adrenaline rush were all working against him. But he didn't have time to stop and worry about that at the moment. First he had to find Daisy.

I can't lose her, he thought, desperate tears burning the corners of his eyes. *I can't. We have to talk about this. She has to listen to me. . . .*

His initial passivity had dissipated, and now all he could think about was convincing Daisy to give him another chance. Too anxious to wait for the elevator, he took the stairs three at a time. A few minutes later he burst into the Wards' suite.

"Daisy!" he shouted hoarsely, rushing over and pounding on her bedroom door. "Daisy, you have to—"

He stopped short as the door swung open before the force of his fists. Stepping forward, he glanced around the room.

"Daisy?"

It was obvious that she'd already been there. The dresser had been cleared of her jewelry and cosmetics, and the neat line of shoes she'd kept against the wall near the window was gone as well. The closet was standing open, a few of the empty hangers still swinging slightly. He must have just missed her.

Dexter sank down onto the bed, breathing hard. So she was gone. He didn't bother to check Jason's room; the silence was enough to tell him he wasn't in the suite, either.

Lying down on the bed, Dexter clawed back the spread and buried his face in the pillow, hoping for some comforting trace of Daisy's scent. But the hotel maids had done their job well, and all he could detect was a faint whiff of detergent and bleach.

For a moment he felt the crushing weight of his old hopelessness returning, settling on his shoulders like a leaden suit of armor. Now what?

The flight.

His eyes popped open and a tiny spark of hope flared up in his heart. He'd almost forgotten—they were leaving Australia tomorrow to make the long flight back to the United States. Mr. Ward had already secured their boarding passes before he left, which meant Daisy would be stuck sitting right beside him for the better part of a day.

That should give me just about enough time to get through to her, Dexter thought wryly. *I hope. . . .*

He closed his eyes, still hugging the pillow tightly. Tomorrow would be a long, difficult day. He might as well try to get some sleep.

. . .

"Thanks for choosing Oceanic, sir. Have a nice flight."

"Thank you." Dexter accepted his ticket stub from the smiling, dark-haired gate agent, then stepped onto the jetway. He had arrived at Gate 23 early, not having anything better to do on his last morning in Australia. Sitting there in one of the uncomfortable seats in the waiting area, he had watched other passengers arrive, from the balding man in the wheelchair to the young woman who looked too pregnant to be flying to the Middle-Eastern–looking guy who kept getting suspicious glances from everyone else.

But in all that time, there had been no sign of Daisy or her brother. Dexter had hung back even after his row was called for boarding, hoping to spot them hurrying in from the airport aisleway. Finally, though, he'd gone ahead and joined the line to board.

Maybe I missed them when I went to the bathroom, he thought as he nodded politely to the flight attendants greeting people as they boarded the plane. *Or when I went to buy that bottled water. They were already pre-boarding when I got back from the snack bar—talk about stupid timing.*

For a second he dared to hope that, when he reached their assigned row, he would find Daisy and Jason already seated and waiting for him. But that didn't happen. The row was completely empty. He bit his lip, glancing around as he shoved his carry-on into the overhead compartment. Flight 815 was a large plane, and from where Dexter was standing, he couldn't really see the people already seated in the rows toward the back.

What if Daisy and Jason changed their seating assignments to avoid me? he thought. *After all, they obviously found a different hotel to avoid me. And the plane doesn't look completely full, so they probably could've made the switch easily enough even at the last minute.*

He sat down in the center seat, automatically leaving the window seat for Daisy. Drumming his fingers on the armrest, he stared blankly at the folded-up tray table on the seat back in front of him and tried to decide what to do.

The more he thought about it, the more certain he became that Daisy had insisted on changing seats. It just seemed like something she would do. All he had to do was walk down the aisle toward the back of the plane, and he'd almost certainly find her.

But by the time he'd psyched himself up to give it a try, the flight attendants were already snapping shut the doors on the storage bins and reminding people to fasten their safety belts. Any searching Dexter wanted to do would have to wait until after takeoff.

As the main door swung shut, Dexter settled back into his seat. Suddenly his stomach let out a grumble so loud that the man sitting across the aisle glanced over in surprise before returning his attention to his book. Dexter grabbed his bottled water, which he'd set on the aisle seat, and took a long gulp of it. He hadn't dared to spend any money on food that day, knowing he would need his last few dollars to pay for the cab ride to the airport. Instead he'd made do with the half-eaten bag of chips Jason had left behind in his otherwise empty bedroom.

I'll get up and check the rest of the plane right after takeoff, Dexter assured himself, screwing the cap back on the water bottle with slightly shaking fingers. *She's got to be on board somewhere—they said there wasn't another flight out until tomorrow.*

Just then he noticed a flurry of activity near the main door.

As he glanced that way it opened again, and Dexter's heart soared. *Daisy . . .* he thought eagerly.

Instead, a very large, very sweaty young man entered. His breath was coming in labored gasps and his curly hair was frizzed out wildly in all directions, but he was grinning as broadly as if he'd just won the lottery or something. Even in his worried mood Dexter couldn't help smiling a little himself as the latecomer lumbered down the aisle, shooting a thumbs-up sign to a kid sitting in the center aisle a few rows away from Dexter.

Once the big guy disappeared into his own seat, however, Dexter's smile faded immediately. He shot a sidelong glance at the empty seat beside him. The door up front was closing again, and this time he suspected it was for good.

She could be back there somewhere already, though, he thought. *She was definitely mad enough at me to switch her seat and sit in coach.*

He waited impatiently while the plane taxied slowly to the runway. It seemed to take forever before their turn came and the flight was cleared for takeoff. Dexter closed his eyes as the plane roared up into the sunny Australian sky, not even bothering to say his usual little prayer for a safe flight. His mind was completely fixated on what he was going to say to Daisy.

By the time the captain turned off the seatbelt sign, the flight attendants were already getting started on the first beverage service. When Dexter looked back, he saw their little metal carts blocking both aisles behind him.

Maybe I'd better wait until they're done, Dexter told himself. *No big deal.*

It was a long flight. He would have plenty of time to work things out with Daisy before they reached their stopover in Los

Angeles. In fact, maybe it was better to give her a little time to cool off before he tried talking to her.

He felt a flutter of relief at the thought of putting off their confrontation. Did that mean he was only making excuses? He closed his eyes, trying not to feel like the world's biggest coward.

Wouldn't it be easier just to forget about the whole thing? a little voice whispered inside his head. *There are plenty of other girls back at school. You could try for one of them. Or you could add another class next semester to keep yourself busy and forget about girls for a while. Maybe you just weren't born to be happy. . . .*

"Something to drink, sir?"

Dexter's eyes flew open, and he saw an attractive female flight attendant smiling down at him. "Oh," he blurted. "Uh, nothing for me, thanks."

She moved on, allowing Dexter to slide back into his gloomy thoughts. His mind spun ahead into the future, and he saw himself wearing a white lab coat, listening to an endless series of faceless, discontented people complain about their problems, and then going home to a barren, lonely apartment. . . .

No, he thought rebelliously, shaking his head to clear away the grim vision. *It doesn't have to be that way. I can still fix things, make everything all right—all I have to do is find Daisy.*

Just as he was reaching for the buckle of his seatbelt, someone hurried up the aisle and flopped into the aisle seat beside him. Startled, Dexter glanced over.

"Yo," Jason said, unsmiling. "What's up, dude?"

"Not much," Dexter replied cautiously. "Um, where've you been? When you guys didn't make it here to your seats . . ."

"Enough with the small talk, man." Jason's face looked puffy and pale; it was obvious he was still hungover from the previous night's excesses. He tugged at the hem of his over-sized basketball jersey. "I just came up here to let you know that Daisy wants you to stay away from now on."

"Where is she?" Dexter demanded.

Jason shrugged. "To be honest with you, man, I don't even know. I'm not sure if she made this flight in the end or not. She changed our seat assignment to get away from you, and we ended up in two single seats in totally different parts of the plane. Then right before pre-boarding, she told me to go ahead without her." He shrugged. "Guess she was having second thoughts about sitting in coach. Can't say I blame her—it sucks back there. Thanks a lot, dude."

Dexter opened his mouth, ready to offer to switch seats. He might not be Jason's biggest fan, but he figured it was the least he could do under the circumstances.

But before he could get the words out, Jason was gone. Dexter slumped into his seat, his recent determination completely sapped by what he'd just heard.

Whaddaya expect, boy? his aunt's voice scolded in his head. *Folks like us ain't made for good things. You oughta know that by now, or you're stupider'n you look.*

He realized he was clutching the armrests so tightly his knuckles were white. How could she be that way? Worse yet, how could he just sit there all those years and let her turn him into the same kind of person? Oh, he might not be quite as out-wardly unpleasant. But he was just as much a victim of her neg-ative thinking as she was. For a while it had seemed he was breaking free by creating his new life as SuperDexter. But wasn't that just another way of being ashamed of who he really was? Why hadn't he trusted Daisy—and the rest of his friends at school—to like him for himself?

Dexter wasn't sure how long he sat there while the self-accusatory thoughts spun through his head like a dizzying roulette wheel of guilt. Nauseating waves of cowardice, passivity, and despair racked his whole body, making his throat and stomach spasm.

Finally, he realized there was just one way to make the pain stop. It was time to take action. Past time, really. He couldn't go on this way; now that his two worlds had collided, he saw that it never could have continued much longer. Even if he could figure out a way to fix his relationship with Daisy, the whole two-lives thing just wasn't working for him anymore.

The passive part of his mind seemed to slip away, as if blown back out across the ocean in the exhaust of the jet engines, leaving him with a new sense of resolve. Whatever happened with Daisy, he couldn't go back.

As soon as I get home, I'm going to do something about the whole situation, he vowed, this time knowing that he wasn't going to wimp out or change his mind. *I'll start by having a serious talk with Mom and Aunt Paula. If they won't let me pick my own major—control my own life and future—then I'm through with them. I'll give back the money and make it on my own.*

He felt nervous but also invigorated by the thought. At that moment, he realized that he'd finally shaken off an entire lifetime of fear and submissiveness.

It was a good feeling, and it gave him the courage to make another vow: *I'm going to make Daisy talk to me, too, no matter what Jason says,* he thought. *She owes me that much. I deserve that much.*

Despite his new sense of purpose, he felt another shudder in his stomach at that thought. But he took a deep breath and glanced behind him. Enough stalling. He was going to search the plane row by row until he determined whether she was on it. If she was, he was going to talk to her and not stop until she listened to what he had to say. And if she wasn't, he would track her down and do the same once they were both back at school.

It's no wonder she's upset now, he thought. *But she's not an unreasonable person. If I come clean, explain why I did it, tell her about my life before I met her . . . Well, maybe there's still a chance for us.*

The idea of telling her everything—no secrets this time, no holds barred—scared him a little. But it also made him feel oddly brave.

He smiled. Then he unfastened his safety belt and stood up, crouching to avoid hitting his head as he slid toward the aisle.

Suddenly the plane lurched violently. The entire cabin pitched and shuddered, the metal framework groaning softly in protest.

"Ow!" Dexter muttered as his head cracked painfully against the overhead compartment. He saw stars, and grabbed the seat back to keep himself from stumbling into the aisle.

The FASTEN SEATBELTS signed blinked on with a *ping,* and the reassuring voice of a flight attendant came on over the PA: "Ladies and gentlemen, the captain has switched on the fasten seatbelts sign . . ."

Dexter sank back into his seat, rubbing the bump on his head. He couldn't help being shaken by the sudden, violent disturbance in the otherwise smooth flight, but it hadn't dampened his determination. He would find Daisy as soon as the turbulence was over.

23

"THANKS FOR LISTENING." KATE shot Dexter a quick glance and a half-smile. "You're easy to talk to."

"No problem." Dexter didn't bother pointing out that he'd done more talking than she had. All he'd been able to get out of her was that somehow, there was a gun on the island. And somehow, someone had used it to put the dying man out of his misery, at his own request.

After that, she'd deftly changed the subject to why he was out in the jungle at that hour. Before he knew it, he'd found himself telling her almost his entire life story.

Now she sighed, staring up at the stars winking down at them from high above the treetops. "It's strange," she said softly. "It can be so hard to talk to people sometimes. Even when you know it's the right thing to do."

"Yeah," Dexter agreed. He shot her a curious look, wondering if she was ready to open up to him a little more. "Who are you thinking about?"

She hesitated for so long that he thought she wasn't going to answer at all. "Jack, mostly," she said at last. "I know I need to talk to him about—about something. Something . . . difficult. It's just so hard to find the right moment."

"Then maybe you need to *make* the moment," Dexter suggested. "If it's important to you to talk to Jack, just go ahead and do it. It probably won't even be as bad as you—"

"What makes you think he'd even try to understand?" she shot back before he could finish, sounding almost accusatory.

Dexter still had no idea what she was talking about, but he shrugged. "He might not," he told her, his mind slipping back to his own problems back home. "But all you can do is try. I just wish I'd tried a little harder to make myself talk to Daisy."

Kate's shoulders went limp, and she nodded. "You could be right," she agreed. "Maybe I'll try to talk to him tomorrow." She glanced over at him. "Sorry. I didn't mean to bring you down with all this."

"You didn't," he mumbled with a twinge of self-pity. "I brought my problems all on myself. Now that everyone knows I've been lying about who I am, they're never going to trust me again. Not that I blame them."

Kate shook her head. "I doubt that. Everyone has secrets, you know." Once again, she stared up at the distant stars. "In a way, being here is a way for all of us to start over. Clean slate."

Dexter glanced at her doubtfully. He suspected she was just being nice. What could someone like her possibly know about his kind of secret life? Still, he appreciated her effort to cheer him up. If she could hear what he'd told her and not seem bothered by it, maybe things weren't so hopeless for him on the island after all.

A few minutes later they headed back to the beach. When they stepped out of the trees, Boone spotted them and hurried over immediately.

"Dexter, dude," he said with obvious relief as Kate faded off in the direction of the fires. "Don't scare us like that! The way you ran off like that, in the dark and all . . . You had us worried about you, man."

"You were worried?" Dexter felt a flush of emotion. "But after the way I lied to everyone . . ."

Boone shrugged and waved him off. "Don't be an idiot," he said. "You weren't yourself—none of us were after the crash, I guess. Plus you had the whole dehydration thing going on."

Arzt hurried up just in time to hear Boone's last comment. "He's right, you know," he said. "I keep telling you, you gotta drink a lot and take care of yourself. What do you expect to happen otherwise?" He sounded annoyed, but his eyes showed concern as well.

"Thanks, guys. Sorry to worry you."

He glanced over and saw Shannon staring in his direction. When he shot her a tentative smile, she gave only a fake-looking half-smile in return before quickly turning away.

Dexter sighed. Okay, so maybe not everyone was going to look at him the same way now that they knew the truth. But he couldn't control that; all he could do was accept it.

"So you guys really aren't going to hold the crazy Dexter Cross stuff against me?" he asked, going for a joking tone and failing miserably.

Boone shrugged. "You can't help what you say when you're not in your right mind."

"Right." Arzt nodded and pursed his lips primly in his best "teacher knows best" expression. "The important thing is that you're telling us the truth now that you've remembered it."

"Thanks, guys," Dexter said gratefully. "And don't worry. It's the whole truth and nothing but from here on out."

A ripple of movement caught his eye over at the edge of the jungle. Dexter glanced that way. Was that a dark, solitary figure skulking there in the trees, just out of the firelight's reach?

His doppelganger turned away, not interested any longer. Whatever was out there, it didn't have anything to do with him.

A little later, he sat beside one of the signal fires with Boone talking things out. "So it's no wonder I couldn't remember that fancy restaurant you and Shannon kept talking about," Dexter commented with a rueful chuckle. "I'd never been to LA in my life until the stopover on my way to Australia."

"So now that you've remembered the rest of your real life, do you remember if your girlfriend was on the plane?" Boone asked.

Dexter shook his head. "I'm still not sure," he said. "All I know is I haven't seen any sign of her on the island so far."

Boone nodded. "That's tough, man."

"Yeah." Dexter sighed and stared into the fire. "So I'll have to wait until we're rescued and see how that turns out."

He was starting to realize that there were always going to be things he didn't know or couldn't understand. Maybe that was how life was meant to be.

And maybe all we can do about it is keep searching for the truth, he thought, rubbing his scar thoughtfully. *Whatever it takes.*